'Marry me.'

Ben dropped into the chair opposite and smiled slowly, raising one hand in a tacit command to silence as the beginnings of a scornful flush crept up from her neckline. 'It would be a mere formality, you understand. A piece of paper. And over just as soon as you deemed it safe to be available again.' He added in a cool, flat voice, 'Think about it. The offer will be open for another twenty-four hours.'

Dear Reader

There's nothing more wonderful than celebrating the end of winter, with an exciting collection of books to choose from! Mills & Boon will transport you to all corners of the world, including two enchanting Euromance destinations—sun-drenched, exotic Madeira contrasting with scenic evergreen Wales. Let the spring sunshine brighten up your day by reading our romances which are bursting with love and laughter! So why not treat yourself to many hours of happy reading?

The Editor

Diana Hamilton is a true romantic and fell in love with her husband at first sight. They still live in the fairytale Tudor house where they raised their three children. Now the idyll is shared with eight rescued cats and a puppy. But despite an often chaotic lifestyle, ever since she learned to read and write Diana has had her nose in a book—either reading or writing one—and plans to go on doing just that for a very long time to come.

Recent titles by the same author:

THREAT FROM THE PAST
LEGACY OF SHAME

SEPARATE ROOMS

BY

DIANA HAMILTON

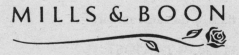

MILLS & BOON LIMITED
ETON HOUSE, 18-24 PARADISE ROAD
RICHMOND, SURREY TW9 1SR

*First published in Great Britain 1994
by Mills & Boon Limited*

© Diana Hamilton 1994

*Australian copyright 1994
Philippine copyright 1994
This edition 1994*

ISBN 0 263 78415 0

*Set in Times Roman 11 on 12 pt.
01-9403-48758 C*

Made and printed in Great Britain

CHAPTER ONE

'Is THIS man bothering you?'

The relaxed, vaguely transatlantic drawl cut Honey's tirade off in her throat. She hadn't wanted to come to this wretched party and Graham, as ever, was being a pain. But she'd imagined her voice had been pitched low enough not to carry, especially considering the volume of chatter. Registering the tide of scarlet that flooded Graham's nicely put together features, she turned on one spiky heel to deliver a frosty comment and met speedwell-blue eyes in a tanned, fantastically masculine face and promptly forgot what she'd been going to say.

'Well?' One sable brow quirked upwards and Honey's fingers tightened in a defensive reflex action as she clutched her unwanted glass of wine against her breast, feeling the cold shiver of the glass against the creamy flesh exposed above the scoopy neckline of her black silk dress.

'Nothing I can't handle,' she got out, her dark brown eyes still spitting temper. 'Graham's a friend and——'

'If you screech abuse to your friends, I would hate to think what you do to your enemies,' the stranger inserted smoothly, his mouth curling. And Honey turned back to Graham. Screech? Had she really? But Graham had disappeared into the crowd and she felt her shoulders loosen with relief. Good.

She could make her excuses to Sonia and slope away. And the smooth voice drawled amusedly, 'Feeling better now? Fine. The poor wimp's slunk off to drown his sorrows so why don't we two crash out of this rabble and have a quiet drink in one of the bars downstairs?'

The invitation was delivered in a take-it-or-leave-it tone that intrigued her, and she tilted her head on one side and back because he had to be well over six feet tall. *Well* over because she stood five six in her stockinged feet and tonight she was wearing four-inch heels. And no one, but no one, had ever called Graham Trent a wimp before. He was the town's most eligible bachelor, his father one of the richest men in the area. He would be furious if he ever found out!

'I don't drink with strangers.' She knew her eyes were full of laughter; she could feel it, and a little light amusement was a darn sight better than the heavy hassle Graham never failed to provide, and the wide rangy shoulders lifted just slightly beneath expensive grey suiting as the smooth dark voice confirmed,

'But you think it might be marginally better than fighting with friends?' He took her glass from suddenly unresisting fingers and put it on a wide window-ledge, those quite incredibly blue eyes smiling down into hers. 'And if it makes you feel easier I'll introduce myself. Ben Claremont, long-time buddy of Colin Watts. I'm a house guest with them for the next few weeks, which is why I couldn't get out of this thrash tonight. And if we don't make a run for it now Sonia's going to grab us.'

Watching his tall, lithe body move effortlessly through the crowd, making it patently clear that he wasn't bothered whether she went with him or not, Honey swallowed a grin and began to follow. Well, why not?

Besides, he had been right. Sonia the indefatigable would soon pounce on any guests who weren't circulating, chattering and grinning to show they were having a whale of a time. And although Sonia had been a friend since schooldays Honey had never been able to understand why every year the Wattses hired the biggest function room in the town's smartest hotel to throw an anniversary party. Everyone knew that the other three hundred and sixty-four days they were at each other's throats!

In any case, Ben Claremont's take-it-or-leave-it attitude intrigued her, she had to admit. She had been fighting men off ever since she had turned seventeen and it was refreshingly different to come across one who was quite obviously not bowled over by a curvaceous body, wicked brown eyes and a mane of fiery red hair!

She caught up with him at the head of the sweeping, thickly carpeted stairs and, apart from the way he dipped his glossy dark head in acknowledgement, he made no comment, merely matching his pace to hers as they descended the shallow staircase, the noise level receding to an opulent hush as he stood aside to allow her to precede him into the discreetly lit and elegantly furnished cocktail bar.

'Make it two cognacs,' Ben told a hovering waiter, then sat on the banquette next to Honey,

his endless legs casually outstretched, his eyes
frankly curious as he followed on, 'What were you
and your friend fighting about, Honey? He looked
as if he wanted to strangle you.'

She gave him a level stare. Did he know her name,
or had he simply been using a meaningless endearment? The only way to find out was to ask.

'How did you know my name?'

'Simple, I asked.' The brandy balloons arrived
on a silver tray and he extracted a note from his
pocket, idly gestured the waiter away, his eyes never
leaving hers as he drawled out a string of par-
ticulars. 'Honey Ballantyne, twenty-six years old,
dealer in antiques, with a sizeable shareholding in
BallanTrent Components. And the dog-housed
boyfriend is Graham Trent whose father has a fifty
per cent holding in the said company. Right?' His
long mouth twitched, registering the black snap of
her eyes. 'And before you blow a gasket, Sonia vol-
unteered the information. All I did was ask who
you were. She tells me she's your best friend.'

Oldest, but not best—Honey's thoughts went off
at a tangent. And trust her to give out her life
history at the drop of an idle question. Sonia had
always been a gossip, a stirrer, and the older she
got, the worse she got. It came from having an
empty life.

The silent spurt of temper he had so obviously
noted was now under control and she leaned back,
her eyes narrowing as she observed the way he
cradled his glass, warming the liquid with his
capable, well shaped hands. He looked supremely
relaxed and at home with himself and she was glad

he hadn't been trying to sweet-talk her, using a meaningless endearment. She was tired of empty flattery from men who only saw her as a sex object. So far, this man seemed different from the many others who had tried to get her into bed and when he repeated, 'Why were you and Graham fighting?' she was sure enough of his impartiality to offer defensively,

'He started it. Going on and on about Sonia's and Colin's fifth wedding anniversary party and how we'd be ninety years old before we got around to celebrating our first. I will not be pressured that way.' Temper surfaced again, had her reaching for her glass, swirling the contents round and round the bowl. And Ben deduced disinterestedly,

'I take it you're in no hurry to name the day. How long have you been engaged?'

'We are not engaged. Never have been and never will be.' Honey gave a sagging sigh and sipped at her brandy, feeling the smooth, expensive liquid slide easily down her throat, beginning to unknot the bunch of tension lodged behind her breastbone. Then she asked with a sharp sidelong glance, 'Why so interested?'

'I'm not—particularly.' His elegant shrug was indicative of indifference. And then he qualified, 'At least, only in as much as I'm interested in people—what motivates them, why they act as they do in different circumstances.'

'Oh?' Her interest caught, Honey took another sip of the warming spirit and bestowed a slight smile. 'Why? What are you—a social worker, a writer, maybe?'

'Much duller.' He returned her smile with a trace of wryness. 'I'm Claremont Electronics. Much the same line as BallanTrent. Boring stuff, as I'm sure you'd be the first to agree.'

Blandly said, but Honey's fine brows drew together. Had Sonia told him of the running battle between herself, her mother and Henry Trent, her deceased father's partner? Could be. Which would explain his comment about boredom. But she'd heard of Claremont Electronics. And maybe that company and BallanTrent could be classed in the same breath, but only just. Claremont was world-wide, huge, and specialised in futuristic stuff, designing and manufacturing electronics for the space industry. A different and far classier kettle of fish... And if he was *the* Claremont, then, by all accounts, he was a near-genius...

'So you're not in love with young Trent and you have no intention of marrying him, am I right?' The rich, comforting voice startled her out of her thoughts and she wrinkled her neat nose.

'Got it in one. Only you try convincing him. I can't. Ever since my mother and his father decided that their sole offspring should marry for the good of the company—all one happy family kind of stuff—he's been driving me crazy. The trouble is,' she confided on a gusty sigh, 'he's so old-fashioned and conventional. The business comes first. It must be secured because it provides not only a sizeable income but social standing, respect, if you like. And if Henry, his father, tells him that our marriage would be the best thing for the dratted business then that, as far as Graham is concerned, is that. Regardless.'

Honey swallowed the last of her drink and crashed the glass back on the table, her movements edgy again. Her temper, always volatile, was in danger of exploding from the pressure she'd been under just lately, from both Graham and her mother, and her mouth curled with derision when Ben put in equably, 'Maybe he's in love with you. Couldn't you put his persistence down to that?'

'Love!' Honey's voice rose several decibels, her magnificent eyes narrowing with scorn. 'Graham loves BallanTrent, his self-image, and golf. In that order!'

'Are you quite sure?' The relaxed voice was smoky, amusement curling through it as the vivid blue eyes roamed from the unrestrained corkscrew twists of her fiery hair to the tips of her elegantly shod feet, taking in every point of interest in between. 'Your mind is alert and bright, your face could be your fortune, and your body is quite definitely of the come-to-bed variety. And don't get me wrong,' he inserted at her suddenly suspicious, withering glare, his tone not altering in the slightest, 'I'm speaking entirely as a non-involved observer.'

'Oh.' The frown between her eyes eased away. Just for a moment she had felt hot and bothered by the lazy sweep of his eyes, the tone of his voice, the things he had said. 'Come-to-bed body' sounded like things she had heard a score of times before and had taken the greatest exception to. But he had shown, all along, his impartiality, described his interest in the situation as merely academic. And even though his arm was stretched casually out along the back of the banquette, his fingers a mere twitch away from the naked, creamy skin of her shoulder, he hadn't once tried to touch.

And his impartiality was back in force when he stated, 'So you are not in love with young Trent and have no intention of marrying him to keep BallanTrent in the family, so to speak. You have repeatedly told him this, to no avail. I take it there is no one else?' And, receiving the quick shake of her head with a tiny smile, he advised, 'You'd better leave the area if you want to get him off your back.'

And Honey fumed, 'Don't think I haven't thought of it!'

'But not seriously.'

How astute. He seemed to know her a little too well for her liking. She got unhurriedly to her feet, smoothing the silky fabric over her curvaceous hips before reaching for her matching evening bag.

'No, not seriously. Why should I? I'm happy here, my business is doing well. Why should I let myself be hounded out of town?' A small, cool smile. 'It's been nice talking to you, but I think it's time I left. Would you make my excuses to Sonia and Colin when you rejoin the party?' No mention of Graham; he deserved no excuses. He would only see them as a type of apology for the way she had goaded, snarled and snapped at him earlier.

She had perhaps revealed too much to this stranger, this man with the clever, incredible eyes. She had always been too ready to trust people, to confide, rarely keeping her own counsel and never bottling her feelings up inside her where they could fester and do damage. A healthy attitude, maybe, but one that had sometimes led her into difficulties.

But not this time, she recognised as he accepted his dismissal with suave grace, walking with her into the foyer and asking, 'Can I order you a cab?'

Relief that he had not, as many another might, insisted on seeing her home flooded her with unreasoning warmth. She gave him a generous unguarded smile, telling him, 'Thanks, but there's no need. I live over the shop, barely a stone's throw away.' She extended a fine-boned hand and felt his own close over it, his fingers warm and hard, the brief contact completely polite, no unnecessary and unwanted lingerings, prompting her to add, 'I hope you enjoy the rest of your stay with Colin and Sonia,' and then, not knowing why she wanted to know, why there was this sudden reluctance to end the conversation, 'Where is your home? I can't quite place your accent. Canada? America?'

'No place in particular.' His shrug was barely noticeable. 'I was born in England but since I finished my education—in the States—I've lived out of suitcases. There's always been some place else to be.'

He looked and sounded bored. With her? Probably. So what? Time she left. One last small and, this time, controlled smile and then she turned on her spiky heels and walked through the revolving doors on to the Cop and made her way up the hill, breathing in the warm spring night air, pushing Ben Claremont right to the back of her mind as she turned into Stony Shut, her heels tapping on the cobbles, her heart lifting as it always did as her shop came into view, the light from the single street-lamp reflecting in the dozens of tiny glass panes of the frontage.

There were dozens of Shuts, or shoots, in old Shrewsbury town, narrow cobbled alleyways leading from one street to another, enabling the pedestrian who was familiar with the passages that riddled the town to get from one end of it to the other in record time. And Honey considered Stony Shut by far the prettiest, the tall, gabled and half-timbered buildings almost meeting overhead; and, apart from the addition of the street-lamp, it must look now as it had looked in medieval times.

Extracting her key from her bag, she let herself in and checked on the security system before threading her way through the overstocked shop. The amber security light gleamed softly against polished oak and rosewood and drew warm glints from her prized display of early pewter.

As always, she was tempted to linger, to gloat over all her lovely things, the things that were hers for such a short time. She always felt a pang when something was sold, which, she acknowledged with a small, self-deprecating smile, was a stupid attitude for a dealer to have. Or a shopkeeper, as her mother called her in that awful, denigrating tone she had taken to using of late.

Honey stopped smiling, checked the bolts on the door to the workroom at the rear of the premises and mounted the narrow, twisty staircase to her living quarters. Tomorrow was Sunday, the day she invariably spent with her mother. She wasn't looking forward to it.

*   *   *

She was woken from a dream which featured a tall, dark man with speedwell-blue sleepy eyes by the insistent shriek of the telephone by her bed. Rolling over, she pushed the long mass of her rumpled hair off her face and fumbled for the receiver, muttering into it, 'What the hell time do you call this?' and heard the affected, breathy laugh, Sonia's gushy voice.

'Nine-thirty, darling. I thought you were supposed to be an early riser.'

Levering herself up against the satin-covered pillows, Honey grumbled, 'Weekdays I am. Sundays I ain't,' but her grumble was forgiving because she was always wide awake by eight on the one day a week she took off from business, even though she'd promised herself the luxury of a long lie-in. Maybe her dreams had made her restless, for some unknown reason...

'So where did you and Ben get to last night?' Sonia wanted to know. 'Graham was furious when he found out you'd sloped away—I thought I ought to warn you. Mind you,' she continued at her normal breakneck speed, 'I don't blame you. If I were a single woman I'd take off with Ben Claremont, no question. He's gorgeous, isn't he?'

Was he? Honey's thoughts strayed, looking back. Yes, she had to admit his looks were fantastic. Not as conventionally good-looking as Graham—but then who would be? she thought sourly—but he had masses more presence, and there was something significantly compelling about those assertive features, those brilliant blue eyes with the thick fringing black, black lashes...

'And he doesn't only excel in the looks department, either,' Sonia was still gushing away.
'According to Colin, he has a brilliant mind and,
of course, he's fabulously wealthy. I envy the
woman who eventually ties him down——'

'He's not married?' Honey got a word in
sideways then wondered why she'd bothered. Ben
Claremont's marital status was no concern of hers.

'No, and hands off! He's my house guest, not
yours!' Sonia giggled. 'I wonder if I could persuade Colin to take one of his precious fishing hol-
idays? In Scotland. Or at the North Pole! No, but
seriously—I just felt I had to warn you. Ben came
back to the party and told me you'd gone home.
You'd had a busy day and were developing a
headache.' Tactful, at least, Honey thought,
glancing at her watch to discover the fingers
marching towards ten o'clock. 'And when I relayed
the message to Graham he was absolutely furious!
You're going to have to come up with a good excuse
for disappearing with Ben and making your
apologies through him and not through Graham.'

'Graham doesn't own me,' Honey pointed out
sharply, not bothering to add that neither would
he. It was a waste of breath. Graham made a point
of acting as if she were his property. Which didn't
do her love-life much good—always assuming she
had the time or inclination to get involved with
anyone. She added quickly, before Sonia could
dispute that statement, 'Thanks for phoning but I
must dash. If I'm late for Sunday lunch Mother
will skin me alive.'

Late or early, Avril Ballantyne would give her a hard time today. Pointing out her foolishness—not to mention selfishness—in refusing to even consider accepting Graham's persistent proposals, Honey thought despondently as she dressed in a softly gathered cream cashmere skirt, tan leather boots and a Cossack-style tawny overblouse, neatly belted around her small waist.

The minimum of make-up—just a smear of moisturiser and a slick of copper-toned lipstick—and she was ready. Leaving her hair loose—'all over the place', her mother would call it—she hitched the narrow strap of her leather bag over her shoulder and made for the stairs. She had given up on trying to please her parent long ago because nothing she did ever seemed to be right. Her father, God bless him, had been just the opposite. She had been his 'Princess' and his death, when she was fifteen, had been the severest, most traumatic blow she had ever had to suffer. Even now, eleven years on, she still missed him.

The phone began to ring as she was halfway down the stairs and she hurried on down, making for the instrument at the rear of the shop. And if it was Graham, itching to vent his annoyance over what had happened last night she would tell him that she never wanted to set eyes on him again, in any conceivable circumstance, and that she would do as she damned well pleased with the BallanTrent shares her father had left her, sell them to whoever offered to buy if she felt like it! And fell over a gate-legged table in her hurry, scattering her display of Victorian pincushions, which gave her rising temper a rapid push upwards, made her voice growly as she snatched up the receiver and fulminated, 'Well? What is it?' to whoever.

'My, my! Did you fall out of the wrong side of the bed, Honey?'

It was quite amazing how that smooth, drawly voice could soothe her. It was like pouring cool ointment on a sore place, she thought as her mouth twitched upwards towards a smile.

'No. Over a table.'

'No harm done?' He sounded as if he cared. Her smile deepened.

'Only to my dignity. What can I do for you?'

Too late, she regretted the loaded question then released the breath she hadn't realised she'd been holding when he didn't take the question as an innuendo and told her, 'It's about the problem you have, the one we were discussing last night. Sonia filled me in on it over breakfast this morning. She seemed to be under the impression that the pressure put on you by various people was too intense to be resisted forever, that you'd end up marrying Trent for the sake of a quiet life. And before you jump down my throat and tell me—probably with justification—to mind my own business, let me tell you that I've come up with a perfect solution to the problem.'

'You have?' Her smile deepened. There was no solution that she could think of, except for sticking it out and refusing to do a single thing she didn't want to do. But she was perfectly willing to listen to what he had to say, even if it meant she was late. She had enjoyed his company last night, the way he'd listened as she'd let off steam, his comments both sensible and objective. It had been years since she'd talked problems over with anyone who hadn't had some kind of personal axe to grind, a biased viewpoint. Not since her father had been alive. He had always encouraged her to bring her worries to him, to talk them out, showing her how to solve her problems logically, his loving kindness never failing to ease them out of the way, put them in their proper perspective.

'But of course,' the dark, velvety voice was assuring her now. 'I'll give you dinner tonight and put the solution to you.'

'That's not possible,' Honey said with a regret that surprised her, considering she hardly knew the man and, in any case, knew his 'solution', whatever it was, would not be worth a row of beans. 'I always spend Sunday with Mother.' If she didn't there would be hell to pay: constant phone calls complaining about loneliness, vague and unconfirmed illnesses—palpitations were the 'in' thing at the moment. 'Can't you tell me now? Or is it a state secret?' she found herself teasing. Most unlike her.

'Over the phone?' His voice was a curl of amusement and she supposed he had a point. Sonia probably had her ear glued to a crack in the door at this very moment, straining to hear every word he was saying in case he let slip something gossipworthy. 'I'll pick you up at seven this evening.'

Somehow, the arrogance of that statement didn't annoy her as much as, on reflection, she felt it should and she merely reminded him, 'You don't know where I live.'

'I'll find out. And don't stand me up,' he warned lightly. 'Or you'll be missing out on an offer I might not be inclined to repeat.'

CHAPTER TWO

OFFER? What offer? What had he meant?

'Sorry?' Honey had to drag her mind away from that strange conversation with Ben and forcibly concentrate on what her mother was saying. For the second time, obviously.

'I was asking you, if you can be bothered to show an interest, whether you thought I'd enjoy a Mediterranean cruise more than my usual quiet three weeks in Bournemouth this year.' Said with barbed patience.

Avril Ballantyne, a well preserved fifty, her expensively tinted pale brown hair worn in the style favoured by the older members of the royal family, clad in a well pedigreed lightweight tweed skirt topped by an oyster silk shirt, looked completely at home in her conventionally furnished luxury bungalow on the outskirts of town, the only jarring notes being the faint frown line between the hazel eyes, the permanently petulant droop of her mouth. Brought on, Honey guessed, by having a daughter who insisted upon being unsatisfactory.

'Why not try the cruise?' she suggested, feeling guilty and hating it. The least she could do while she was here was give her mother her undivided attention, forget Ben Claremont and his supposed solution to her problems and the offer that, apparently, was part of it. 'It would make a change;

21

you've been to Bournemouth for the last five years running.'

'Well——' the droop of the mouth became more pronounced '—it would be nice to have a change. But I've grown used to the permanent staff at my hotel in Bournemouth and I know the town like the back of my hand—all the decent shops and so forth. Little things like that are important when one is on one's own.'

Honey swallowed a sigh and offered brightly, 'Why don't you ask Henry to go on the cruise with you? You've always got on well together and he hasn't had a holiday since Moira died—and that was four years ago.'

'Oh——' Avril fluttered her beautifully mani-cured hands '—I don't know whether I feel up to organising such a venture...' and let her voice tail off into vague confusion.

Honey stared at her, her eyes wide. Her mother had a talent for organising everything and everyone around her that was almost unbelievable. She had turned it into an art form. The only thing she hadn't been able to organise was the way Honey chose to run her life. And her mother picked herself out of her apparent distressed confusion, saying, 'I don't know why you should think Henry, not to mention myself, could begin to think about taking a holiday when your behaviour recently is hurting and worrying us so much,' and Honey decided cyni-cally that all roads led to Rome, didn't they just, her mouth tightening as Avril ploughed on, 'Henry simply can't understand why you're treating his son so badly. And frankly, my dear, neither can I. Any normal young woman would jump at the chance of marrying into the Trent family,' she stated, her voice beginning to rise. 'Graham has so much to offer. I can't think what you've got against him. He's exceedingly good-looking and very steady. He'd make a wonderful husband and father, and——'

'I'm sure he would,' Honey cut in, sick to death of the topic. 'Only I don't want him. Call me abnormal if it makes you feel any better. But I don't love him.' She was trying hard not to lose her temper, an exercise that was probably good for her soul, she tried to tell herself, and forced a bland smile as she rose to her feet, offering, 'I'll clear away the lunch things while you relax.' Escaping to the kitchen to do the dishes would be easier to bear than listening to her mother going on and on about Graham, wouldn't it just? 'And then how about we go for a drive in the country? We could finish up with a meal out somewhere, my treat.'

Recalling the way Ben had said he'd pick her up at seven, she gave a tiny sigh. He had sounded so definite about it, so sure of her compliance. He'd have a long wait, but that wasn't her fault. If he chose to disregard the way she'd explained about her regular Sunday visits to her mother then he couldn't blame her if he had a wasted evening, could he?

Even so, there was an emptiness in her she couldn't quite define as she tackled her usual Sunday afternoon chore but she plastered a warm smile on her face as she stowed the last of the dishes away and headed back to the lounge.

'Ready? Where would you like to go?' It was a lovely spring afternoon and anything would be better than sitting here enduring the inevitable disapproving monologues. A pootle round the countryside might take her mother's mind off the way her only daughter chose to 'work in a shop', the way she obstinately refused to 'settle down decently with Graham and do the right thing by her dear dead father's company'. As if her father would have scorned her chosen career! He had always advised her to decide what she wanted and then go out and get it. And it was he who had taught her to love and respect the world of antiques, taught her to identify the excellent from the merely good, the acceptable from the dross.

'I don't feel like going anywhere.' Avril laid aside her glossy magazine and put a plump hand on her bosom. 'As you know, I haven't been feeling well just lately—all this worry over the business . . .' Her voice tailed off pathetically and Honey sighed and sank down on to the end of the over-stuffed settee.

'The business is fine, as you very well know,' she pointed out. 'Henry and Graham see to that. Henry's brainwashed you into thinking that the only thing that can hold it together is a marriage between your sole offspring. And the only thing that's worrying you is my refusal to do as I'm told. That, and your desire to have a daughter who sits quietly at home, properly married to her husband's career, bearing his children and entertaining his business colleagues and golfing cronies and ironing his bloody shirts!' Her voice had risen and she made an effort to rein in her temper, explaining more quietly, 'And the only thing that's worrying Henry is the shares Dad left me. Henry himself holds fifty per cent and you and I the other fifty between us. And, at the moment, you never question any of his decisions and neither do I because I don't know a component from a carpet sweeper. Your loyalty to his management will never be in any question, he knows that. But mine? Who knows? I might decide to sell my shares, mightn't I? The premises next to my shop will be going on the market within the next month or so. I would like to expand. I need to expand——'

'You wouldn't!' The powerfully indignant protest gave lie to the earlier excuses of ill health and Honey bit back a smile, shaking her head.

'Only if I could find the right buyer, someone with BallanTrent's best interests at heart. And admit it——' she fixed her parent with a level look '—that's what Henry's so afraid of, isn't it? He wants BallanTrent kept entirely under his control, in the family. That's why he's been bleating on about marriage for the last twelve months. Don't forget, he told me himself that when—when, mind you, not if—Graham and I married the shares I own would come under his control because, as he piously pointed out, I had no knowledge of the business. And that,' she ground out, aware that her volatile temper was threatening to explode, 'would have been enough to make me dig my heels in and refuse to do any such thing—even if I had been head over heels in love with his dull son!'

The genuine sheen of tears in her mother's eyes helped Honey back into a state of control and her voice was softer as she queried, 'Were you and Dad in love when you married?'

'Of course we were—what a thing to ask!'

'And you were happy?' Honey pressed, earning herself a tart,

'Very. We had our disagreements, what couple doesn't? But, in the end, they weren't important.'

'Because you loved each other,' Honey made her point. 'Would you really want to see me tied in a loveless marriage? Would you? And how long do you think it would last? We'd end up hating each other in no time at all.'

'I'm sure Graham's very fond of you,' Avril defended. But there was a cornered look in her eyes that made Honey believe she was at last beginning to win her parent round. But Avril fluttered her hands and grumbled, 'I simply can't understand why you're so against him, that's all. I can think of half a dozen young women who would be only too happy to be his wife.'

The conversation had gone full circle and Honey was in no mood to endure any more. She knew from experience that when her mother was in this mood she wouldn't let the subject rest and wondered, fleetingly, if Graham had reported the quarrel they'd had last night back to his father and if Henry had been on the phone to Avril this morning, grumbling about her daughter's lack of good sense and grace.

She got to her feet and collected her bag. If she stayed any longer she would lose control of her temper and, no matter how much her mother sometimes irritated her, she didn't want a fight on her hands.

'As you don't feel up to doing anything this afternoon, I'll go back and get on with some paperwork,' and managed to keep her smile pleasant, her voice light as she countered Avril's snippy,

'But you always stay on for supper,' with,

'Usually, not always. I do have a business to run. I'll phone you in the week.'

Guilt and relief waged a battle as she drove back into town but by the time she'd parked her car in the lock-up she rented and walked the few hundred yards back to Stony Shut relief had won. She would not be made to feel guilty because she had walked away from a fight in the making, or because she refused to contemplate marriage to a man she didn't much like, let alone love.

She threw herself into the backlog of paperwork with a will and only stopped to make herself a pot of tea and carry it down to the desk she used at the rear of the shop, picking up the phone to remind Fred Wilson that she would be gone before he arrived at nine in the morning, on her way to a country house sale in Cheshire.

Giving herself a moment's grace, she sipped her hot tea and reflected, as she often did, on how lucky she'd been to find Fred. A year ago, almost to the day, he—and his wife, Mary, she was to discover— had walked into the shop carrying a Georgian sofa-table between them. He was a big, blunt-featured man in his fifties, and his first words had been a no-nonsense, 'How much?'

'You want to sell?' Honey was already casting her eyes over the clean, graceful lines, noting that one of the legs was not original. However, the piece had been beautifully restored, the repair difficult to spot unless one knew what to look for, and, if the price was right, she had a customer who was looking for just such a table.

Her pleasure was not even slightly dented by the middle-aged man's blunt, 'We wouldn't have humped it halfway across town if we hadn't.'

'The piece is yours?'

It was a question that had to be asked but she instinctively knew the couple were honest and quite forgave the man's growled, 'Well, it didn't fall off the back of a lorry.'

'Fred—really!' his faded companion admonished, her worried eyes on Honey's as she explained, 'My husband has always collected antiques and, well, as he was made redundant eighteen months ago, we thought we ought to part with some of them.' Fred gave her a withering glare but she met it without flinching, stating, 'There's no point being proud, is there? Anyway, the house is bulging at the seams; we could do with a bit more space.'

And more money in the bank, Honey thought sympathetically. The proud Fred would be unlikely to find employment at his age when so many younger men were desperately seeking work too.

Straightening up from her inspection, she offered a price that was as generous as she could viably make it, telling them, 'It's the best I can do. I suppose you know the table's been restored at some stage of its life? But the quality of the work is such that it doesn't affect the value too much. I don't suppose you know who restored it?' There was always a slim chance that they did, that they—in more affluent days—had commissioned the work. The restorers she used weren't altogether reliable and, just lately, their prices had begun to soar. So if——

'Fred did.' There was real pride in his wife's voice. 'It's been his hobby for years—buying damaged antiques and doing them up. He's always been good with his hands.'

'In that case——' Honey gave the blunt-featured man a huge grin '—why don't I make us all a cup of tea and we can discuss business?'

Which was how the talented Fred Wilson had come to work for her, performing his magic in the workroom at the back of the shop, looking after the customers for her on the days when she attended sales. She didn't know what she would do without him now...

Returning her cup to her saucer, Honey gave her attention back to her work. Soon deeply engrossed, the tapping on the shop door didn't impinge at first, but when it did her mouth went dry. Looking beyond the circle of light shed by the desk lamp, over the dark shapes in the dim body of the shop, she could just make out the black silhouette of a threateningly large male outside the small-paned windows.

She should have turned on the interior lights ages ago, activated the alarm system, she thought uselessly, then took herself in hand. Felons didn't knock to announce their presence, fool! she told herself. She got to her feet, reaching for the light switch, and remembered.

Ben. Of course. Despite what she had told him he had said he would come at seven. And he had. A rapid glance at her watch confirmed the time and she was smiling idiotically as she went to let him in. Relief. She was just pleased she hadn't a weirdo, or something worse, on her hands. That was all.

'So you changed your plans, after all. Sensible lady.'

His smile was as smooth as cream as he walked through the door and waited while she shot the bolts home. And in case he got the wrong idea, believed she'd done so for the pleasure of sharing a meal with him, she explained coolly, 'I wasn't expecting you, actually, not after what I'd said. I left Mother sooner than I'd intended because if I'd stayed we'd have been at each other's throats.'

One dark, well defined brow drifted upwards. 'Your unspeakable silliness regarding the gorgeous Graham, no doubt?'

'Something like that.' Honey relaxed enough to offer him a wry smile. He had a calming effect on her and, although he was a virtual stranger, she felt more at ease in his company than with anyone else she knew. And she watched, her brown eyes warm, as he strolled among her things, lingering in front of her collection of early pewter displayed on a six-teenth-century carved oak chest.

'You have some fine pieces,' he approved at last. 'You can tell me how you came to get started over dinner.'

No mention of his promised solution to the problem of Graham, she noted drily. Not that anything he could have dreamed up would have helped, of course, but knowing that it had been an excuse to date her left a nasty taste in her mouth. She had, in the past, been dated by experts, men who had, in various ways, let it be known that they regarded dinner for two as an unobstructed pathway into her bed. This man was smoother than most, though, more devious. But his intentions had to be the same.

The disappointment was so intense that the withering look she gave him took even her by surprise and her voice was frozen acid as she refused.

'I'm working. I have no plans to go out to dinner.'

His mouth twitched.

'You still have to eat and we don't need to go out. In fact, it's probably better if we stay here, we have so much to talk about.'

'We have?' Honey's mouth curled cynically. The few dates she'd been misguided enough to invite into her home hadn't been into conversation. But the derisory tone of her voice rolled off him as if it had never been there in the first place and his long, strong fingers were already unfastening the buttons of his obviously tailor-made soft leather jacket.

'Sure.' The fingers stilled and, for some unknown reason, she couldn't tear her eyes from them. He had beautifully crafted hands. They mesmerised her. 'If it's any help, I could go out for a takeaway.'

His afterthought was softly considerate and
Honey denied throatily, 'No. There's no need.' And
watched those fingers deal with the remainder of
the buttons and swallowed hard. Somehow, she
seemed to have committed herself to spending time
with him, cooking for him, inviting him against her
better judgement into the sanctuary of her home.

She didn't quite know how it had happened.

Leaving him to wander around her overstocked
showroom, she activated the security system then
turned and watched him, her head on one side. Had
he really tried to figure out a solution to the
problems she was facing from her mother, Graham
and Henry? And if he had, why had he bothered?
She was simply a woman he had met at a party, he
hardly knew her at all, so why should any problems
of hers be of the remotest interest to him?

Or had he simply used it as an excuse to get her
on her own? And if he had, it shouldn't worry her.
She knew how to signal a pretty formidable 'hands
off' message. She'd had plenty of practice. Besides,
he hadn't shown the tiniest flicker of sexual interest
last night . . .

'You need more space.' Ben eased himself between a jewellery showcase and a mahogany
bachelor chest, that unique, relaxed smile of his
softening his utterly masculine features and Honey
smiled back because with this man she couldn't help
it.

'Tell me something I don't already know. Shall
we go up?' And she was still smiling as she led the
way up the twisty stairs and he was just as easy to
talk to as she remembered from the night before

because by the time they had finished the pasta with tomato sauce he had helped her prepare in the tiny kitchen she had told him her life story, such as it was.

Blabbermouth, she sniped at herself, but was too relaxed to be really annoyed with the way her tongue ran away with her. But so far he hadn't told her a single thing about himself and she leaned back in her chair as he divided the remaining Côtes du Rhone between their two glasses, determined to remedy the situation.

'So what brings you to this neck of the woods?' she asked, easing her boots off beneath the table. 'You tell me Colin's an old friend—you must have a lot of catching up to do to be staying with them for weeks on end.' She couldn't have stood to be Sonia's house guest for a few days, let alone a few weeks, old friend or not. She was not a peaceful person to be around; she never stopped talking, for one thing.

And Ben must have read her thoughts because the smile he gave her was like a secret shared, then he stretched out his long legs beneath her table and told her, 'I'm setting up a production unit in the new industrial park on the edge of town. I like to take charge of the whole operation personally. Colin offered me bed and board and I took him up. I've spent too much time in hotels.' He picked up his glass and drained the remaining contents and Honey grabbed her cue.

'I would have thought you'd have got around to having a home of your own by now. You sound as if you could be described as a person of no fixed abode.' She was fishing, she knew that. But she was curious. He knew everything there was to know about her, or almost, and she knew next to nothing about him. And she didn't know why, but she wanted to know everything.

But he appeared not to have heard her comments. Slewing round on his chair, he ran his eyes over the room. Fairly large, heavily beamed, three small casement windows overlooking the Shut, the stone hood of the fireplace finely carved with strange heraldic beasts. And he said, 'If you moved out of here you could use this room at least as a second showroom. And presumably you have a bedroom? Large enough to act as a third?'

He turned the full and shattering force of his sleepy sapphire-blue eyes on her and Honey's readily volatile mood swung from relaxed enjoyment to blistering contempt. As a hint it was definitely unsubtle. Did he really think she was about to invite him into her bedroom, invite his opinion on its suitability as an extra showroom? Did he think she was that stupid or that eager to round the evening off in the way most men seemed to take for granted?

'I don't think my shortage of space is your problem, do you?' She gave him a ferocious look, her fingertips drumming on the table. 'And while we're on the subject of problems, what was the grand solution you were supposed to have dreamed up?' Snapping brown eyes challenged lazy blue and she saw his mouth twitch and wanted, quite desperately, to hit him, her ruffled feelings not much soothed by the even tenor of his drawled,

'Do you always fly off the handle so easily,
Honey? Did you really imagine I introduced the
subject of your bedroom because I couldn't wait to
leap on you? Nothing, I solemnly assure you, was
further from my mind. I was simply making
conversation.'

Which should have soothed her but somehow
didn't. Apart from the annoyance of finding he
could read her mind he was telling her he didn't
find her remotely attractive, that wild horses
wouldn't drag him into her bed. But that shouldn't
make her feel all turned inside-out, should it? On
the contrary, it should be reassuring, making his
company nice and safe and comfortable. Ever since
she'd turned seventeen her dates hadn't been able
to keep their hands off her, so it was really something to find a man who didn't find her sexually
attractive, who was interested in her chosen career,
who preferred to talk rather than cavort between
the sheets.

So why did she feel so... piqued?

And her voice was gritty as she came back, beginning to gather the dishes, 'Let's forget the polite
conversation bit, shall we? Why don't you toss that
solution at me, then leave?' She made an elaborate
display of consulting her wristwatch, almost
dropping the plates in the process, saving them by
a whisker, adding pointedly, 'I have to make an
early start in the morning.'

'Marry someone else.' He took the stack of plates
from her, putting them gently back down on the
table. Which was astutely self-protective of him,
she fumed to herself. The utter stupidity of his

so-called solution had sorely tempted her to hurl
the china at his head.

But the bubbling beginnings of temper abated to
a simmer and then disappeared altogether. It had
nothing to do with the mesmeric quality of his glittering, vivid blue eyes, she assured herself. She was
at last learning to handle her volatile temper, that
was all. And there was almost a smile in her voice
as she told him, 'I can see such an action on my
part forcing our Graham to back off for good.' She
flopped down in the chair she had vacated and
watched him begin a leisurely pacing of the room.
'However, as there's no one around I want to marry
the idea's a bit of a non-starter, wouldn't you say?'

He had reached the casement windows and his
lean, tall, black-clad body was dominantly sil-
houetted against the cream velvet curtains and he
turned slowly on the balls of his feet, his features
almost austere in the dim lighting as he trod slowly
back to where she sat, his hands in the pockets of
his trousers, emphasising the narrow, sexy cut.

Suddenly, Honey's mouth went dry and her heart
tripped over itself. He looked, as he paced towards
her, like a dangerous animal intent on its prey. But
the brief and unprecedented moment of girlish
trepidation was wiped out of existence as he offered quietly, 'Marry me.' Then dropped into the
chair opposite hers and smiled slowly into her pale-
skinned, open-mouthed face, raising one hand in
a tacit command to silence as the gradual beginnings of a scornful flush crept up from her neckline.
'It would be a mere formality, you understand. A
piece of paper to get Graham Trent finally off your

back. And over just as soon as you deemed it safe to be available again. I'm willing, if you are,' he added in a cool, flat voice. 'Think about it. The offer will be open for another twenty-four hours.'

CHAPTER THREE

OH, BUT he was a cool customer... Cool and calculating. Honey slammed the door of the lock-up and huddled deeper into her raincoat, dragging the hood up over her bright head.

Today had been a total waste of time. Too many London dealers had gathered at the country house sale, outbidding her on each and every item she had wanted. And spring had done a U-turn, making the day gloomy with chilling rain. And, more annoying still, she hadn't been able to drag her mind away from Ben Claremont and his crazy proposal.

Crazy or calculating?

A man would have to be out of his mind to propose a paper marriage to a woman he hadn't known existed until twenty-four hours ago. Out of his mind or on to a good thing!

But what? What could he gain from such a marriage? Honey simply couldn't begin to guess. Her shoulders hunched against the rain, the high heels of her boots beating an angry tattoo on the cobbles, she turned into Stony Shut and for once the warm glow of light coming from the windows of her shop failed to take the edge off her aggravation.

If only she could stop thinking about him, about his odd proposal, about the way he'd simply said goodnight, politely thanked her for the meal and walked away leaving a thousand and one questions racing round her brain.

It wasn't as if she had any intention of accepting his insane offer of a 'solution'—even if he had been serious about it, she grumbled at herself. So why couldn't she get it, or him, out of her mind?

'Honey——' The masculine voice was thin and irritated and she lifted her head, screwing her eyes up against the rain and groaned a disgusted protest. Graham. All she needed right now was Graham.

He was approaching from the other end of the Shut and even in the gloom of the wet afternoon she could see his face was pinched and tight, almost completely eradicating his film-star good looks. He looked about as pleased with life as she was, and if he'd come to ask her to apologise for her behaviour on the night of Sonia's party he would have a long, long wait.

She was nearer the shop premises than he, and dived into the shelter of the doorway, waiting for him, her teeth clamped together, her hands on her hips, like a warrior defending her kingdom. But his peeved expression had to have more to do with the way the rain had slicked his hair to his head, was dripping off the hem of his stuffily styled shortie car-coat and soaking his trousers than any of her numerous—to him—shortcomings. Because his tone was conciliatory in the extreme as he peered into her bristling brown eyes and told her, 'I've come to bury the hatchet, old thing.'

'Wow! Make my day. What have I done to deserve such a treat?' she growled, willing him to go away. All she needed right now was a hot soothing bath, a nice cup of tea and the opportunity to unknot her mind. But sarcasm was wasted because Graham stepped into the shelter of the doorway with her, stoically smiling.

'Don't be like that, sweetheart. That spat the other night was as much my fault as yours, I freely admit it. So let's put it behind us, shall we?' The film-star smile flashed again, the effect slightly diminished by the drop of rainwater on the end of his too perfect nose. 'I've booked a table for two at the Crown. I would have given you more warning but when I phoned this morning that odd-job man of yours said you'd be out all day. I just dropped by on the off-chance you'd be back—otherwise I would have left a message.'

'I don't——'

'I won't come in just now,' he cut across her, as if an invitation to do just that had been extended. 'Must dash. But I'll pick you up at eight.'

'No.' Honey recognised that look in his eyes. It meant he was about to honour her with one of his totally unremarkable kisses. She backed away, knocking into the shop door, her voice tight with temper as she spat, 'You don't give up, do you? I won't have dinner with you tonight, or any other night. So why don't you go back home and tell your father to keep his nose out? I won't marry you, because I don't want to. And, if you think about it, you don't really want it either.'

But he was still smiling, as if she were a bad-tempered child who didn't know what she was talking about. Still advancing, too. And she had nowhere to go but into the haven of her shop and she was already fumbling for the door-latch when it swung open behind her, sending her toppling into a strong pair of arms—another kind of haven.

'You always fall into my arms so beautifully, my angel. That's just one of the things I love about you.' The relaxed and slightly amused tone of Ben's voice calmed her and the strong arms around her body warmed her, dispelling the memory of the chilling rain. Graham's face was a picture of outrage and she closed her eyes because Graham's face was not what she wanted to see, and nestled her head into that broad, accommodating, soft-leather-clad shoulder. And heard his voice assume a cool toughness. 'Is there anything we can do for you? The premises are about to close and, as you can see, my fiancée needs to get out of her wet things.'

Which brought Honey's eyes flying wide open again, and she could swear her heart actually stopped beating for whole seconds. And it wasn't a reaction to the words Ben had said, oh, no, just a frantic need to see how Graham took that 'my fiancée' bit.

If he actually believed she was engaged to this suave stranger then surely he would drop his own pursuit, the desire to fall in with his father's wishes and marry the woman the cunning old man had picked out for him. It might work, it just might work, and if it did she would treat Ben to the best meal the Crown could offer, the best champagne too, by way of celebration.

But luck wasn't riding with her because Graham's face had gone black with temper and his voice was more incisively confident than she had ever heard it before as he bit out, 'As you said yourself, Honey——' he invested her name with a kind of disgust '—I don't give up. And there's no way I'm going to let some smooth-talking Yank take my woman.' His eyes snapped with a ferocity she wouldn't have believed him capable of as he swung on his heels and delivered his parting shot, 'And you'd better believe it. Both of you.'

'Oh, heavens!' Honey's bright head burrowed more deeply into Ben's wide shoulder, the tangle of her damp curls brushing his tough jawline. She might well have stayed there forever had he not gently put her aside, she recognised with a grumble of self-disgust when he brushed drops of water from his jacket and said wryly,

'Quite a determined guy you're up against there.' Then, his eyes taking in the rain-darkened cork-screw twists of her hair, her dripping raincoat and sodden boots, he told her crisply, 'Time to get out of those wet things,' and closed the shop door behind them, flicking the 'Open' sign to 'Closed' and dropping down the latch.

'Any luck today?' Fred ambled through from the rear of the premises, his craggy face bright with interest because usually, after a sale, they drank mugs of tea together and discussed the treasures she had found. But not today.

'No, nothing.' Honey shook her head regret-fully. 'The big boys from London were there *en masse*. I didn't stand a chance.'

And Ben put in from right behind her, 'Just as well. You couldn't cram another teacup into this

place and still have room for customers to browse.'
He edged past her, making a production of it as if
to prove his point. 'Get those wet clothes off and
take a hot shower while I brew coffee. We'll lock
up, Fred, if you want to call it a day.'

Bossy, she thought as she watched him stride to
the twisty staircase at the back of the showroom.
But there was no resentment there, just an unusual
willingness to allow someone else to take charge for
once. Someone? Or just this one man?

She shrugged unconsciously and lifted long
sweeping lashes to meet Fred's twinkling eyes.

'There goes a man who's used to getting his own
way. It comes naturally, and it shows,' he said with
the same lack of resentment.

In fact, Honey noted, his expression was
thoroughly approving and she brushed wet,
wrinkled hair out of her eyes and asked weakly,
'Just how long has he been here?'

'Long enough to get the business straightened
out.' Fred was already reaching for his ancient
sheepskin coat. 'He thinks you should move out
and make your flat over to extra display areas.
Forget the idea of buying up the next-door
premises—the structural alterations to throw the
two properties into one would totally destroy the
character of both. I agree with him.'

'Really.' Honey's voice was withering as she
watched her right-hand man shrug into his coat.
Ever since they'd heard that the adjacent property
was due to come on the open market they'd avidly
chewed over the possibilities of acquiring it, ex-
panding the business—always presuming she could

raise the capital. And now, just because some sort of bossy nomad had wandered in off the street, Fred had, in his mind, evicted her from her cosy home. So where was she supposed to live? Move in with her mother? Heaven forbid!

She would have reminded him that this was her property, her business, and she—and no one else—would decide what was done. But her sharp little tongue was silenced by Fred's jaunty, 'See you tomorrow, then. Pity about the sale. Night.'

'And goodnight to you, too!' Honey sniped at the already closing door, then turned slowly on her heels, the damp cloth of her raincoat making her shiver. What the hell? Nothing to get in a stew about. It hadn't been a good day, that was for sure, and the unpleasant encounter with Graham, out there in the driving rain, had been the last straw.

All she needed to recapture her normal optimism was that hot shower and a hot drink. And if Ben wanted to produce the drink why should she argue? Just so long as he didn't offer to scrub her back!

As she went to her bedroom she could hear him moving around in the kitchen. She would have liked to ask him to leave but couldn't rake up the energy. The long day, the frustration of the sale, the nasty knowledge that Graham wasn't about to abandon his pursuit—even though Ben had said they were engaged—had sapped her strength.

So she wouldn't think about any of it. Not now. After her shower, after Ben had taken himself off, would be soon enough.

Divesting herself of her wet clothes, she tugged on a short scarlet silk robe, belting it securely at the waist and padded out of her room—meeting Ben in the tiny passageway. Suddenly, for no reason she could think of, she felt her face go as red as the silk that clung to every curvaceous line of her body. But he didn't even seem to see her. He looked straight through her as he imparted briskly, 'Good girl. I'll have dinner ready in half an hour.' He almost smiled. 'Come as you are, no need to dress for the occasion.'

Huh, she snorted to herself as she shed her robe in the privacy of the tiny bathroom. No need to dress. Come as you are! Was that a build-up to a pass, or wasn't it! Her face going hot, she rushed to bolt the door and immediately felt silly. He hadn't even seemed to see her out there, and he certainly hadn't subjected her to the lascivious slide of the eyes that meant he was mentally undressing her. She had been on the receiving end of just such looks for years now and was perfectly capable of recognising them.

Annoyed with herself for her mental over-reaction, she stepped into the shower and allowed the soothing spray of hot water to relax her and was almost tempted to do as he had said—present herself for dinner in her robe—but thought better of it and pulled on a pair of washed-out jeans topped by a baggy sweatshirt in a faded shade of black that seemed to emphasise the paleness of her skin, the delicate lines of her triangular face and the wildness of her rough-dried, shoulder-length vivid red hair.

Though what he had found to cook was beyond her. She knew for a fact that her fridge was empty, the store cupboard shelves bare of the makings of a meal. She had been too busy just lately to be bothered about such trifles as grocery shopping.

So the aroma of sizzling steak coming from the kitchen was a complete surprise, as was the sight of Ben Claremont with a tea-towel tied around his lean waist, his strong angular features frozen in a mask of concentration as he flipped the meat over then slid it back beneath the grill.

Then the mask dissolved into a smile of such warmth that Honey found her breath snatched away, her voice just for once totally lost as he put a cup of steaming coffee in one of her hands, a small measure of brandy in a tumbler in the other.

'Go and warm through by the fire.' He gave her an absent-minded push, turning her round, his hands on her shoulders, very briefly, not lingering. He surely didn't appear to be the mauling type, she thought in a haze. True, he had held her quite intimately when she'd fallen into his arms as the door to the shop had opened, but that had been purely for Graham's benefit, a physical back-up to his roundabout announcement that they were an engaged couple. He had certainly lost no time in putting her aside as soon as the other man had stumped away in a rage.

And it hadn't been Ben's fault that Graham had taken the so-called engagement news as a direct challenge. He had tried to help her. So she wouldn't bristle at him because he had taken over, pushing her out of her own kitchen, giving orders.

Besides, she would find it impossible to be angry. He had an uncanny knack of soothing her. Well, some of the time. Like now, with the fire he had made burning brightly in the hearth, the flames throwing dancing shadows and splashes of glowing colour over the ancient carvings on the stone hood, the hot coffee and tiny sips of brandy relaxing her.

The table they'd used last night was already set with two covers. He'd certainly been busy while she'd been taking that shower and when he entered with a platter of steaming steak with fresh asparagus on the side, a bottle of champagne tucked under one arm, she smiled at him dreamily and uncurled languorously from the squashy armchair at the fireside.

It was nice, for a change, to be cosseted. No one had done so since her father had died; no one had petted her or really cared about her and what she wanted, or treated her as if she was important, special to them. Not even her mother. Especially not her mother! Avril had only been interested in having a daughter who would conform to her ideas of what a daughter should be. Honey's personal wishes were disregarded if they didn't dovetail with Avril's—as witnessed by the endless arguments over her decision to set up in business on her own, by her refusal to do the sensible thing and give it all up to marry Graham!

The sound of the cork popping, the crisp foam of bubbling magic into cold crystal reminded Honey of her earlier intention to treat him to a celebratory drink and, a quirky smile playing around her mouth, she seated herself at the table, spread her napkin over her lap and told him, 'Thanks for trying to give Graham the red light. It's a pity it didn't work, but you can see what I'm up against.'

Giving a minimal shrug, Ben served her food and slid one of the foaming glasses over the table towards her, his tough features bland as he agreed, 'He's got more determination than his weak chin would have led me to expect, but then the weak can be remarkably stubborn. But that's no real problem, as I see it. Eat your food.'

Taking a sip of the cool, crisp champagne, Honey had to agree that Ben was right. Now she came to think of it, Graham's chin did have a habit of disappearing completely at times. She cut into the tender steak, all at once feeling oddly light-hearted, and imparted sagely, 'Our fathers were partners, you know, and as Graham and I were both only children I think it was always hoped we would get together one day. At least, that's what Mother, Henry and Moira hoped—Dad would never have pushed me into anything I didn't want to do. He was an absolute sweetie.'

The loss, which could still hurt, even after eleven years, showed fleetingly in her eyes and Ben put in softly, 'Your father meant a great deal to you, didn't he?' as if he knew all about the closeness that had existed between them. 'And who is Moira? Henry's wife?'

'Was,' Honey corrected, cutting more meat. 'She died about four years ago. She and Ma were always pushing Graham and me together. Parties, picnics, the tennis club—you know the sort of thing. And after she died Ma and Henry must have got their heads together and put the pressure on. And

Graham was very nicely brought up, brainwashed into doing every damn thing his father told him to because it was "right". Hence the futile pursuit. If I've told him—not to mention Henry and Ma— once, I've told him a thousand times. I will not marry him!'

'Quite right, too!' Ben placed his cutlery together on his empty plate and lounged back in his chair, one arm hooked casually over the back, his other hand curled around the stem of his crystal flute. 'And were you "nicely brought up"?'

Honey's eyes laughed into his over the rim of her glass. Talking to this guy was really easy; he seemed so interested in what she had to say.

'Difficult to say. Ma certainly did her best. But Dad wasn't so much interested in the way I dressed, the way I spoke, the children I mixed with, as in the way I thought. He taught me to be independent, to ask questions, to find out what was going on in the world beyond our small village.' She ran the tip of one finger round the rim of her glass, her dark eyes reflective, her voice barely above a whisper now. 'He started taking me to galleries when I was five years old, to the opera and theatre when I was six. I'll never forget those weekends in London as long as I live. He taught me to appreciate so much—it was he who taught me everything I know about antiques, not only by visiting the big showrooms in the capital, but local sales, too. And, of course, at Folly Field we lived with beautiful things year in, year out.

'Don't ask me how the house got that name— Dad didn't even know. But it had been in his family for generations and he loved it as much as I did. After he died, Ma sold it and the contents—every last thing. And I went a little wild. Uncontrollable, she said. What with losing Dad and Folly Field in one black stroke I became a very pernicious adolescent!' Her voice had tightened and her eyes flickered with the temper that had been her way of coping with the stress of her double bereavement. God, she had let her tongue run away with her again, revealing far too much to this cool, laid-back man! she thought, livid with herself.

'One thing your father didn't teach you was how to control that temper,' Ben remarked idly, his vivid eyes wandering in an almost disinterested way over her now hectic cheeks, the lush lips that were pressed together in a hard, tight line. 'It's probably irremediable, like the red hair.'

'Oooh!' The impulse to strike him was strong, to slap that slightly patronising, slightly superior expression off his face. But she made a conscious effort to control the desire and he said gently,

'Have some more wine,' refilled her glass and brought her right back to the present, suggesting, 'Why don't we discuss the offer I made last night? A mere engagement isn't going to put Graham off; he demonstrated that much earlier on. The only way for you to get rid of the irritation is to marry someone else. Me. And, as I told you, it would be a mere formality. Of course——' speedwell-blue eyes glinted into hers '—we would have to live together, appear together from time to time. That goes without saying. So, I would have to buy or rent a house in the area. This place——' he

dismissed her beloved flat with an eloquent shrug
of wide hard shoulders '—is far too small to contain
us both and is totally inadequate for the business
entertaining I would need to do if I settled around
here for any length of time.'

Honey glared at him with stony eyes. She had
actually forgotten about his lunatic proposal. The
wine, the brandy, the food, the rare feeling of being
cared for and pampered had made her put his stupid
offer right to the far reaches of her mind.

He hadn't been pampering her, making her feel
special at all. It had all been calculated—everything—just a softening-up process to induce her to
accept his offer of marriage! Disappointment hit
her like a knife-thrust. She couldn't speak, so she
gritted her teeth and glared at him instead, her mind
churning sickeningly as he drawled, 'But living
together wouldn't mean I would make any sexual
demands on you at all. Quite frankly, my dear, you
don't turn me on. And, provided you were discreet
about it, I wouldn't object to your...seeing
someone else, if you felt so inclined. And of course
I would expect the same liberty in return.'

'Get lost!' Honey yelled bitterly, springing up
from the table, upsetting her wine glass, which
rolled to the carpet with a dull thunk. Laying her
hands, palms down, on the smoothly polished
wood, she leant forward, eyeball to eyeball, her face
quite white as she glared into his spectacular features, empty of any expression except a flicker of
mild amusement. So she didn't arouse the slightest
hint of sexual interest in him, so as far as he was
concerned she was one big turn-off! And he

wouldn't lay her if she happened to be the last woman on earth! Yet he would marry her and take dozens of lovers—discreetly, of course—and she could do the same and he wouldn't give a toss! Oooh! 'And you can take your foul offer with you, and——' Words failed her, clogged her throat and he simply smiled at her with brilliant eyes and she thought, even above the raging of her brain cells, that she detected a note of satisfaction in the sultry voice.

'You obviously need more time to think it over. Tomorrow? The arrangement would work in both our interests.' He stood up with the indolent grace that was beginning to infuriate her, reaching for the leather jacket he had tossed on to a sofa much earlier. 'You know where to find me. Think calmly, and phone me tomorrow.'

He was already on his way to the door. Honey stared at him across the debris of the meal he had prepared and felt unaccountably empty, her anger evaporating, leaving a strange sense of desolation behind. The fire had burned low in the hearth and an odd kind of loneliness squeezed her heart. And although she knew she didn't want to know, and she most assuredly didn't want to keep him here for one more second, she asked quickly, 'What would you get out of it? You don't even like me! So why would the "arrangement" work in your interests, too?' Because he wanted a paper wife, a paper marriage? Because he couldn't or wouldn't commit himself to one partner for life? With a wife in the background he could have as many affairs as he liked and none of his women could make serious demands on him.

Oh, yes, she had quite made up her mind and was utterly prepared to hear him confirm her dark suspicions. But what he actually said was worse, far worse, in her opinion, and she could only toss her fiery head in disgust as he calmly told her, 'To hang on to my inheritance. My grandfather owns the larger part of a Greek island, a beautiful villa— not to mention interests in various businesses on the Greek mainland. The old man hasn't long to go. In fact, he's failing rapidly, so I believe. He has threatened to disinherit me unless I marry and settle down. The whole of his estate will go to his man-servant unless I marry within the next month.' He placed his hand on the doorknob. 'When his secretary wrote to put the old man's stipulations before me a couple of months ago I was resigned to losing all that. Unlike my grandfather, I don't find any appeal in the married state. The very thought of saddling myself with a wife and a bunch of children gives me a pain in the gut. But a marriage such as ours would be, which would last only as long as necessary, would be tolerable.'

He was really on his way out now and Honey could only stare at him with contempt. What a louse! As if, with Claremont Electronics, he didn't have enough wealth and power already! Greedily, he wanted more. And didn't care how he got it!

And, for the moment, he stared back, quite remorselessly, then gave her his devastating grin.

'I said you didn't turn me on, Honey—not that I didn't like you. I do. You're quite a woman.'

And left. Just like that. And Honey didn't know whether to scream and stamp or not. Not, she finally decided, determined to be dignified, no matter if she felt like exploding. And dignified she was as she raked out the ashes of the fire, washed the dishes and tidied up and took herself to bed. And didn't sleep. Not a wink.

'I'll be gone for about an hour, Fred,' Honey said, and swept out of the shop in the middle of the following afternoon. She had to think and she knew where she had to go and her little car had covered the ten miles out of town to Folly Field without her seeming to have anything to do with the proceedings.

She had tossed and turned all night, wrestling with her conscience, trying to push Ben's offer of marriage right out of her head. But her brain kept coming up with sneaky little asides, reminding her of what a strain fending Graham off had been for the last goodness only knew how long. Not to mention all the aggro she'd had from her mother. That really didn't bear thinking about. If she upped and married someone else all that would stop. Immediately. And would a marriage in name only— *stress that*—be so bad? True, she would have to share the same roof as the louse but she needn't have much to do with him. A little business entertaining, a few social affairs—well, she could handle that, couldn't she? And the way he would be deceiving his grandfather wouldn't be on her conscience, would it? Besides, any man who could make such a dogmatic stipulation when it came to finalising the details of his will had to be power-crazy. And possibly deserved all he got. There certainly didn't seem to be much affection flying around between Ben and his grandfather.

The 'For Sale' notice planted beside one of the stone gateposts at the head of the long driveway to her former home was, after six months of winter weather, considerably faded. And because the lovely old house was empty now, the people who had bought from her mother all those years ago having moved out when it had first been put on the market, Honey drove up the drive, noting the sprouting weeds with disfavour and parked firmly in front of the rambling stone building.

She hated to see the house empty, but she had hated to think of other people living here and once, when she had driven out, visiting the tiny post office in the nearby village to demand to know what precautions were being taken against vandalism now that the property was empty, the fat old postmistress, who had known her all her life, had stated, 'Oh, the police make regular checks in one of those squad car things and the locals keep their eyes open. Mind you, the things some young tearaways get up to nowadays... You should buy it, get it back in your family where it belongs. We hear your business is doing well in town.'

Buy it. If only she could. Although her business was doing well, it wouldn't pay the price needed to get Folly Field back.

And now the house was looking deserted indeed. Honey could hardly bear to look at it. Leaving her car, she stalked around to the rear of the house, averting her eyes from the overgrown lawns, the rank, last year's weeds that smothered the once beautifully planted borders and sat on the stone bench in the walled courtyard where she had played so happily as a child, never dreaming that the day would come when she could no longer call this lovely old house her home, when her father would no longer be around to guide, encourage and love her.

What advice would he have given her? To take the opportunity to rid herself of Graham once and for all, to put an immediate and effective stop to all the insidious pressure Avril, with no conscience seemingly, was putting her under? Or to bear with it into the foreseeable future?

And there was no answer. She would have to make up her own mind. Somehow. She closed her eyes and leaned wearily back against the sun-warmed wall.

She walked briskly back through the shop an hour later. Fred was busy with a customer. She gave him a tight smile and went on up to her flat. Her shoulders were ramrod-straight as she punched in Sonia's number, her voice crisply controlled as she asked to speak to Ben. And when his deep, drawly voice came on the line she gave a tiny shiver as something deep inside her unknotted and sent electrifying sensations through every cell in her body, then, frowning at her own reaction, hauled herself together and said just two words.

'I accept.'

Then put the receiver back on its rest and felt as if an enormous burden had been taken from her shoulders.

CHAPTER FOUR

THEY were married three weeks later, very quietly in the local register office. And as the registrar's voice droned on Honey made all the right responses, but her mind was far away.

Avril had wanted a church wedding, all the trimmings, but Honey had put her foot down. It would have seemed like sacrilege and, besides, the arrangements would have taken too long. Only she and Ben and a dying old man on a Greek island knew why speed was of the essence.

For once, though, her mother hadn't sulked at being thwarted. Indeed, after the initial shock when she and Ben had told Avril of their plans, the latter had become surprisingly acquiescent. Something to do with finding out who Ben Claremont actually was, Honey thought cynically, remembering the pleased glint in her mother's eye as she had pronounced, 'Well, the dear boy's a better catch than Graham, I'll say that for you. And it's time Henry learned that he can't have things all his own way. He'll have to be satisfied with his fifty per cent holding in BallanTrent, won't he? After all, he and Graham will still make all the decisions, just as before. And I think I'll book myself on to that cruise, if I haven't left it too late.'

So why couldn't she have taken that attitude months and months ago? Honey thought now,

staring into space. If she had, she, Honey, wouldn't
be standing here, being legally tied to this tall, dark,
impeccably turned-out stranger.

She shifted uncomfortably on her spiky-heeled
bronze shoes, oblivious to the intense blue gaze of
the man at her side. She was marrying Ben
Claremont and she hardly knew him at all, and the
little she did know she didn't like! She would, she
recognised, feel better about the whole thing if
everyone else had disapproved! But the way her
mother had eagerly welcomed Ben 'to the family',
her arch smile sickening from where Honey had
been standing, had made her feel uncomfortably
guilty. Even Henry had given her a grunt of approval, to her total amazement. And although Ben's
parents hadn't been able to come over for the ceremony his mother, Fanny, had phoned from their
home in California sounding, to Honey's guilty
ears, like the warmest, most friendly soul in the
universe.

'Wouldn't you know it? Our only son—that
workaholic wanderer we thought would never settle,
let alone marry and give us the grandchildren we're
itching for—has finally found himself a lady and
named the day. And we won't be there! Ed's booked
in for gall-bladder surgery two days before your
wedding—just like a man! But our thoughts, all
our love will be with you every second of your big
day—you can count on that!'

She had sounded almost tearful as she'd passed
Honey over to her husband, and Ed had added his
good wishes, good-humouredly repeating Fanny's
statement that if they didn't get themselves out to

California at the very first opportunity he and Ben's mother would come and fetch them. Just see if they didn't! They couldn't wait to meet the little lady who had finally pinned their boy down. She must be quite something!

Which had made Honey feel ashamed of herself. Everyone seemed so happy, everyone believed it was a case of love at first sight. Sonia had gone quite tearful and vowed it was so romantic that she was going to die of envy. Lie right down and die!

If only they knew. Her reason for marrying—to get out from under the continual pressure from Avril, Henry and Graham—had been base enough. But Ben's was worse. She supposed the 'rapidly failing' old man, out on his Greek island, had received the telemessage announcing his grandson's compliance with his stipulations and had done the right thing; that the inheritance was now safe. She hadn't asked. She didn't want to know. Even her natural curiosity, her sharp little tongue, had been stilled by the sheer enormity of what she had agreed to.

During the last three weeks she had felt only half alive, not even able to show any interest in the home Ben had rented for them on the banks of the Severn, one of an early Victorian terrace built above the flood-line with a tiny garden in front and a tinier one behind, scooped out of the hillside. Two up and two down with the usual offices, it was pretty enough, but scarcely much larger than her own flat, the flat Ben had, in his lordly fashion, derided as being too small for the lavish entertaining he seemed to think necessary.

She had been too flattened by the weight of her sins to bother to question his choice and she gave a gusty sigh, suddenly feeling too hot and contricted in the tawny silk suit she was wearing, the nipped waist of the collarless jacket too tight, the skirt too narrow, too short.

And felt her wooden little face cupped by the warm palm and long fingers of an unmistakably masculine hand, the inescapable fingers turning her head, positioning her just so. And then the dipping movement of his head, the brush of his mouth against hers. Just a light movement across her cold lips at first, and then the return, the warm opening pressure that made her mouth quiver beneath his, the slow slide of his tongue that was a secret between them sending her brain off into orbit. It was the first time he had kissed her; her body knew that and was astonished by the effect, and her mind told her that it would be the last because the murmur of congratulations informed her that the ceremony, if it could be called that, was over. They were now man and wife.

Honey felt quite dizzy. Ashamed of herself, too. Ashamed of the way his kiss had affected her when all it had been was an act for the benefit of the others. Ashamed to accept all those congratulations, the good wishes of the guests. And how was she supposed to get through the lunch party that was to follow? And how would she be able to smile and pretend this marriage had been made in heaven when it had been made in hell?

Alarmingly, adrenalin spurted through her body and she knew, she just knew, that any moment now she would get panic-stricken and leap out of the building and run down the street like a demented thing, scattering her teeter-heeled shoes, her silly hat and her small bouquet of apricot roses in her wake.

But Ben's hand tightened on her arm, almost as if he knew what was going on behind the wide brown eyes, and she suddenly went all limp and dispirited again and sagged weakly against the hard, sinewy strength of his splendid body.

'How nice,' Honey said in a polite voice as the landlord of the small hotel showed her her room, then turned to escort Ben to his, further down the corridor. Separate rooms.

Separate rooms, and she wouldn't have it any different and she was only feeling sombre because this wasn't what she had imagined her honeymoon would be like. Two days at a small Welsh coastal resort, just two days because, as Ben had explained to interested parties, he couldn't afford to be away for longer, not while the arrangements for the new business set-up were going full steam ahead. Later, they would take time to have a proper honeymoon.

Lies, all lies, like everything else about this sham of a marriage. He simply saw no point in spending time with his new bride when there was plenty of work waiting for him back home. Two days in her sole company would be as much as he could stand.

And that went for her, too, didn't it just! Her expression moody, she dumped the small suitcase she had brought with her on to the big high bed and wondered if she could be bothered to unpack.

'Comfortable? Do you have everything you need?'

Just the sight of him, the sound of his voice, sent Honey into a dither. He had walked right in without bothering to knock and that was not to be tolerated. Stormy eyes glared at him. He was leaning back against the door, regarding her quizzically, a tiny smile tugging at one corner of his sensual mouth. And he was wearing light grey trousers topped by a casual black sweater. So he had changed, and she could have been in the middle of doing just that when he had barged in.

The thought made her face go red, even though a delicate shivering sensation was attacking her legs and making her feel insanely weak all over. And it was all his fault and she told him crossly, 'In future don't simply walk into my room. Knock.'

'Afraid I'll see something I shouldn't?' One dark brow curved wickedly upwards. 'I wouldn't see anything I haven't seen before, and I doubt if the sight of you *au naturel* would send me mad with lust.'

He levered himself away from the doorway and paced slowly to her side and Honey hated him. So he didn't find her in the least way fanciable. Fine. Right. But did he have to keep rubbing it in?

'Nevertheless,' she muttered tartly, 'we have to lay down some ground rules,' and compressed her lips as he sat on the bed, testing it for comfort.

'This seems fine.' He tilted his dark head, ignoring her comment, blindingly blue eyes watching her pale triangular face. 'And I repeat, do you have everything you need?'

His eyes were like jewels in the severe mascu-linity of his face. They mesmerised her. She tore her gaze away and fastened it on the clean but dreary wallpaper, her lips barely moving as she ground out, 'Everything except my privacy.'

'Oh, dear! Why so uptight, I wonder? Apart from a few patches of stormy water we rubbed along remarkably well before today.'

Even though she refused to look at him she could feel the steady assessment of his eyes, hear the dry note of mockery in his voice. She had enjoyed his company, had found him easy to get on with, easy to talk to. And he was one of the few men she knew who had not put her under any kind of sexual pressure. But that had all changed and she snapped right back, 'We rubbed along, as you call it, until I accepted your hateful proposal. After that I de-spised you.'

'Ah—I see now. I thought you were quietly con-taining your gratitude for my rescue package and all the time you were despising me.' He swung his endless legs up on to the bed and leaned back against the pillows, his arms crossed behind his head, and Honey opened her suitcase and began to thrust the contents willy-nilly into a chest of drawers, ignoring him. But she couldn't ignore his mocking taunts; they made her skin crawl with self-loathing.

'And did you despise yourself when you found friend Graham backing off? When you finally did something your mother could approve of? Or were you too busy despising me for making it possible? And were you too busy thinking dark thoughts of me to call the whole thing off? You could have backed out, you know. Right up until the last minute.'

She didn't know why she hadn't. She didn't know why she had agreed to this farce in the first place.

Up until meeting Ben Claremont she had been very firmly in charge of her life. The pressure on her to marry Graham had been a constant she had been able to cope with. True, there had been times when she had contemplated packing her bags and setting up in business somewhere a long way away, but those times had been mere hiccups and she had always known she could cope, would carry on in her own sweet way, regardless.

So why she had agreed to take up the offer of an easy way out she couldn't fathom. It troubled her. Especially as it was beginning to seem that it wouldn't be easy at all.

There wasn't an answer, not one she could find, and she would have left him to it, left him to toss his taunts into an empty room, gone down to the tiny reception area to find someone who could produce a tray of tea, but Ben swung lithely off the bed and sauntered over to the window.

'Come here.'

She was at his side before she had time to wonder why she had so mindlessly obeyed. But she kept a careful distance between them, holding herself stiffly, knowing she was behaving childishly because she had gone into this marriage with her eyes wide open, but unable to do a thing about it even though she desperately wanted to project a cool and sophisticated image.

'Closer. You can't see the view if you don't look.'

But her feet were mutinously rooted to the floor and at the faint sound of his irritated indrawn breath she flicked him a quick sideways glance and saw the compressed line of his mouth just before his arm snaked out, curving around her waist as he physically hauled her closer.

This close to him she felt very vulnerable and the warmth of his hand burned her flesh through the thin silk of her suit and only when he released her, which he did very quickly, could she even try to focus on what he wanted her to see: a picture-postcard view of a curving sandy bay sheltered by hump-backed cliffs which descended rockily into the dancing blue-green sea. And, in the crinkled green valley, a straggle of cottages linked by narrow, steep lanes invited exploration.

Ben told her, 'It used to be a smugglers' paradise, so the bumf from the Welsh Tourist Board would have us believe. In any case, much of the coastal land is owned by the National Trust, which means we can get some unrestricted cliffs walks in while we're here. The fresh air should help deal with today's stress.'

He walked back into the body of the room and her wide brown eyes followed him. So today's sham had been a strain for him too, had it? Could he be regretting the lengths he had gone to to secure his inheritance? Did he have a conscience after all? If so, she could get back to liking him again, couldn't she? And suddenly the quick little tongue that had been frozen for all these weeks came back to life and she confided, sounding breathless, 'I know what you mean—everyone thinks our marriage was the romance of the decade when it's anything but. I feel so deceitful. I hate it!'

He shook his head slowly, his dancing eyes warm on her earnest face and it seemed to her that he was going to come back to the window where she stood, to say something to make her feel better about the whole disgraceful charade. She was so sure of this that she felt beautifully warm inside but all he said was, 'People believe what they want to believe, and how we conduct our marriage is our affair. Yours and mine, Honey. Now, why don't you get changed?' He was already making for the door. 'We've enough time before dinner to take a look at the village and walk on the beach. See you downstairs.'

Dragging disappointment kept her where she was for a full three or four minutes. She had been so sure he had been about to console her, tell her that what they had done was not dishonest, not too abnormal, that they wouldn't be the first people to use the married state as a convenience and they assuredly wouldn't be the last. That they were friends, bound by the marriage contract, that something deeper could grow out of friendship, couldn't it?

The lump in her throat brought her back to her senses and her pale face was furious as she began to get out of the suit she'd been married in. She didn't know what had come over her, she truly didn't. She didn't want something deeper to grow, of course she didn't. For one thing, she wasn't ready for a permanent commitment; she was committed full-time to her business. And even if she were ready for a full personal relationship it wouldn't be with him!

Meanwhile, of course, they had to get through the next weeks and months, for as long as it took for Graham to get permanently involved with another woman and for Ben's grandfather to...

Angrily, she blanked out the rest of that thought. The next few months would be hell on earth if she continued to remind herself of how despicable Ben was. It would be easier if they could be polite to each other during the time they were forced to spend together.

So the façade she presented was at least dignified as she joined him in the small lounge set aside for residents. Thin on the ground at this time of the year, of course, but no doubt the place was bulging at the seams later in the season.

Taking her cue from him, she had dressed casually. But the fine needlecord jeans in a vibrant shade of scarlet were eye-catching, she acknowledged, clipping her curvy hips, neat bottom and nicely rounded thighs with perhaps a little too much loving care. And the cream-coloured sweatshirt she had teamed with the jeans actually did nothing to lessen the impact.

Maybe she should learn to tone down her normal flamboyant style of dressing, she thought worriedly as she hovered in the doorway. But she needn't have felt even the slightest bit apprehensive because when Ben lowered the paper he'd been engrossed in and rose fluidly from the depths of one of the armchairs his impressive features were completely impassive, his sapphire-blue eyes totally uninterested, only acknowledging her change of apparel with a laconic, 'Ready, then? Or would you like some tea before we set out?'

'No, thanks.' Her tone had been brusque to the point of rudeness and she was already regretting that as she turned to stalk out to the lobby. Dressed as she was, with her vivid colouring and curvy figure, her appearance would have drawn admiring glances—to say the very least—from any other man on the planet, as she knew from long and aggravating experience. But he could have been looking at a sack of coal!

He had already told her he didn't find her even slightly attractive, she reminded herself as she walked out on to the narrow lane in front of the inn, feeling his eyes on her back. And that, she assured herself, was a huge bonus. It meant they could cohabit in peace, that she wouldn't have to dodge a sneaky pair of hands, endure the assault of a lustful pair of eyes, or fight off a rampant male who had decided—despite their agreement—to demand his conjugal rights!

Dragging in a deep breath of salt-laden air, she closed her eyes briefly and vowed to curb her impulse to snap at him. He had treated her with politeness and she must try to reciprocate. It was the least she could do. And she had a smooth, innocuous remark concerning the idyllic position of the inn he had chosen for their stay hovering on the tip of her tongue when his hand clamped around her arm as he frog-marched her down the lane towards the bay, his voice dry as he wanted to know, 'Who the hell named you Honey? I would have thought Vixen would have been far more appropriate.'

The metalled lane had given way to a sandy track by now and Honey dug her heels in, incensed. And once again she closed her eyes, fighting the impulse to scream at him, to slap his hand away from her arm. Hadn't she, mere seconds ago, vowed to keep their relationship, such as it was, politely distant?

A shuddering breath later, she swallowed her ire and turned to him with a brilliant, empty smile.

'Let's keep personalities out of it, shall we? The next few months will be far easier to get through if we keep everything impersonal and businesslike.'

Slowly, his hand fell from her arm and a little wind gusted in from the sea, making her shiver, tossing the red corkscrew twists of her hair around her head like a cloud of fire. And his eyes went dark and hard but his voice held no inflexion whatsoever as he said, 'You're probably right. I stand rebuked,' and walked away, finding the firmer sand near the water's edge, bending now and then to pick up a stone and skim it over the bouncing waves.

Honey trudged in his wake, fuming a little, wondering if she should keep her head subserviently bowed, wear a veil over her face, maybe? And when he deigned to remember she was around—if he ever did—how should she react then? Bow her head until her nose touched her feet?

And even when he did remember his encumbrance, it was only to offer his hand to help her up the steps that had been carved into the rock and which led, in one direction, up to the cliff path and, in the other, to the village.

She ignored his hand. She was quite capable of clambering up a few steps unaided, thank you. And she couldn't help narrowing her eyes to a glare as he told her coolly, 'We'll leave the cliff walk until tomorrow, take a packed lunch. But we've enough time to take a look round the village.'

'Oh, my! I do hope I don't get too over-excited!' Honey breathed, a comment he chose to ignore as he strode—all wide black-covered shoulders and long, lean legs—down the narrow main street which tended to wind all over the place and branch off in the most unexpected places. At least he didn't ignore her, but it was probably worse than if he had. His comments about the age of the small stone church, the quaintness of the sole village shop, which seemed to sell everything from galvanised buckets to frozen fish fingers, were impersonal, polite and bland enough to make her want to scream and rake her fingers through her hair, making it wilder than it already was.

Normally, she knew, she would have been delighted by the charming village, by the way the stone cottages were perched at various levels all along the narrow, tree-filled valley, entranced by the little gardens already brimming with spring flowers. But nothing, it seemed, could soothe her mood on this day, the most disastrous day of her life, she decided with a strange upwelling of some inexplicable emotion.

And even dinner, back in the comfortable atmosphere of the inn, accompanied by a surprisingly good bottle of wine, did nothing to help her unwind.

She couldn't fault his manners. He was polite to the point of painfulness. 'Impersonal' simply wasn't in it! And if he made one more bland remark about the freshness of the grilled sole they had been given or the state of the nation, she would hit him!

Glancing round the cosy, firelit room with a narrowed glare, she felt as if she were in prison and wondered if the handful of other diners, locals, she guessed, felt the same. And knew they didn't.

And Ben wouldn't be feeling trapped, either. He had secured his inheritance—albeit one he couldn't possibly need—and enduring her company was the price he was perfectly willing to pay. She drank the remains of the wine in her glass in one long swallow then turned her strained attention to her coffee, stirring the spoon around the cup until most of the contents washed out on to the saucer and Ben said softly, his mouth curling with hateful, untroubled amusement, 'You'll wear a hole in the bottom. Stop making a mess and drink it nicely.'

As if she were a graceless child!

With enormous self-control, Honey replaced the spoon in the brimming saucer and rose to her feet. Her legs were shaky but she ignored that and said very slowly, because if she spoke quickly she would begin to gabble and then, in all probability, to shriek, 'It's been a tiring day. If you'll excuse me, I'll go to bed.' And made herself ignore the excruciatingly annoying quirk of his gorgeous mouth, the pin-points of amusement in his fantastic eyes and forced herself to walk calmly out of the room, her head held very high.

But once out of there she took the stairs two at a time, stormed into her room and banged the door, leaning against it, shaking all over.

Oh, but he was hateful! They would keep their relationship businesslike and impersonal, she'd told him. And he'd taken her at her word, gone beyond, far beyond. His politeness bordered on contempt and his method of being impersonal trod the precarious line between outright dislike and plain old-fashioned boredom. And if their so-called marriage had to last more than a few weeks she would go quite noisily crazy!

Hating the way her heart was crashing around as if trying to jump out of her chest, she pulled in a deep breath and told herself to be sensible. She had known what she was doing when she'd agreed to marry him and if he was making her feel more churned up than she could have believed possible then she would simply have to learn to cope with it, wouldn't she?

Her room boasted a washbasin but there was only one bathroom on this floor, as the landlord had explained when he'd shown them to their rooms. This wasn't a top-class hotel in a big city, it was a small old-fashioned inn with more ramble than rooms.

And Honey was going to have that bathroom, and hog it until she had managed to unwind. Grabbing the nightdress she'd stuffed into a drawer, her wash-bag, she scuttled into the bathroom and bolted the door. It was lovely and warm, with a deep green, deep-pile carpet and the fittings were gratifyingly modern, the bath deep and almost wide enough to take two. And if this had been a real honeymoon, then it would have been put to the test . . .

Honey squashed that thought immediately and turned on the taps, tipping a reckless amount of her favourite bath oil into the steaming water. And lay in the scented depths for ages until she felt the very last of the tension seep out of her body.

So perhaps she would be able to sleep now, she told herself as she climbed out and wrapped herself in a huge towel plucked from one of the heated rails. Though what had possessed her to pack the slinky white satin thing with its revealing lace halter-top she couldn't imagine. It was an unworn Christmas gift from Sonia, who obviously didn't believe in flannelette modesty.

She couldn't have been thinking straight, if at all, when she'd plucked it from its pristine tissue wrappings and thrust it into her case. It was the type of garment no woman would wear if she were sleeping alone. The type of slinky nonsense that would end up beneath the bed and not in it!

Honey rubbed condensation from the full-length mirror and her face went pink. Really, she looked like a woman who was waiting for her lover—all ripe sensuality, and then some!

But there was absolutely nothing at all she could do about it and as the hotel couldn't be said to be bursting with residents she could surely make it back to her bedroom without being seen.

No point in struggling out of the wretched thing and back into her day clothes before taking the three paces across the corridor to her room.

With her clothes clamped to her chest she lowered her fiery head and began her scuttle to safety—and cannoned straight into a wall of warm muscle and bone and didn't need to wonder who it was because every last tiny, insignificant cell in her body knew.

'I was beginning to think you'd comandeered the bathroom for the night,' Ben said laconically. But there was nothing laconic at all about the way the palms of his hands were touching her naked shoulders with languorous stealth and definitely nothing laconic about her reaction.

The bundle of clothes lay scattered on the floor now and as his hands held her at a breathless distance away from his white-robe-clad body there was nothing between them but the night-dimmed light in the quiet corridor and the slow burning pressure of his eyes.

The balls of his thumbs were describing soft circles on the inward curves of her shoulders, just below her collarbone. Honey was transfixed. It wasn't the pressure of his hands that was holding her immobile, because there wasn't any pressure, not really. It was the sensation, the stunning sensation; that and the slow drift of his eyes as they ate up the way white satin clung to the soft swell of her tummy, the long curving line of her hips and thighs, the way her full breasts were barely hidden at all beneath the filmy covering of lace.

As she felt her breasts peak and harden her mind went into a spin, her soft lips parting to say a crisply decisive goodnight. But there weren't any words there, none at all, nothing but the astonishing pounding of the blood in her veins and self-betrayal came in the form of a small choked sound at the back of her throat and in the way she couldn't tear her eyes away from the triangle of bronzed, hair-roughened skin of his impressive chest, exposed by the short white robe he wore, the long muscled nakedness of his legs.

And his eyes, as she lifted heavy lids to meet them, were wicked and Honey went hot all over, far too weak to resist when his hands slid down her back then fastened on her waist. Burning heat seared through the thin satin, searing her quivering flesh, creating a wild turbulence that was translated into sheer madness as he dragged her into the hard curve of his body.

She was going up in flames, she knew she was, her whole body on fire, her brain already burnt out, a tiny pile of grey ash and no use to her at all. She was being consumed by him and there was nothing she could do to prevent it happening, nothing until he spoke in a rough-edged husky voice.

'You've been as brittle as a shard of broken glass all day; is this what you wanted, Honey?' Hands moved erotically over satin-clipped buttocks, pressing her more tightly into the hard arch of his pelvis. His voice thickened, a growly murmur of knowingness. 'Will this make it better?'

For a moment she went very still. Like a stone. Then her brain cells sprang back to life. Ohh . . . Hateful, hateful man! Near panic, she pushed him away, her lower lip trembling just a little as she told him furiously, 'Never! We have an agreement, remember? I fell against you in the dark, that's all!' She tossed her head, her steam-dampened hair twisting riotously, her triangular face even paler than normal. 'And you took advantage! Don't ever do that again!'

She bristled away with as much hauteur as slinky, body-skimming white satin afforded, crashing the door to her room back on its hinges, and turned, ready to scream her lungs out when he followed her. But all he said was, 'You forgot these, my little nest of vipers.' And tossed her clothes in behind her, the wash-bag following and landing squarely on her bed. 'We don't want someone tripping over them in the night, do we?'

He was laughing at her, damn him! Not openly, of course, but laughing inside, she knew he was. His eyes betrayed him. She hated him. One day she would kill him!

'Go away,' she ordered, tight-lipped, horribly disadvantaged by the sexy nightwear. One day she would kill Sonia, too!

'Immediately, oh, vinegary one.' He dipped his head, a manufactured subservience that didn't fool her at all. His sexy mouth was quirking unforgivably and amusement curled the edges of his voice as he told her, 'I apologise for my mistake and suggest we forget it ever happened. Sleep well, Honey.'

And closed the door quietly behind him and left her staring at the blank panels of wood, wondering how she would ever forget the way he had made her feel.

CHAPTER FIVE

'IT'S spectacular!' Honey's dancing eyes swept over the new showrooms. Oh, it was good to be home, good to be busy! And, oddly enough, she didn't feel the slightest pang at the loss of the living quarters. All her treasures were displayed to the best advantage now instead of being cluttered and bunched together downstairs.

'You've got furniture polish on your face and dust in your hair and you look worn out,' Fred said dourly. 'I'll brew up and then you can get off home. It's late.'

Honey waved him airily away, her smile blissful as she ran loving fingers over the back of an Edwardian *chaise-longue*. She didn't feel in the least tired; it had been a wonderful day. Leaving Ben eating breakfast, she'd walked the half-mile from the riverside house to her shop and thrown herself into the excitement of getting everything sorted.

The removal firm who had packed up her effects, installing them into the house she and Ben now shared, while they had been in Wales, had provided two burly souls to carry and coax the pieces from her overflowing shop up the twisty stairs to what now were her new showrooms. And, added to all the dusting and polishing, the positioning and re-positioning, they had had an unusually brisk day's trading.

Which was lovely. Everything was lovely. And if she had her way she would stay here all night, just making sure that everything was as it should be, just gloating! She wanted to cling on to this euphoric mood, enjoy it. Going back to the house she was sharing with Ben would destroy it.

But she utterly refused to think about him now, and she could always take a bundle of the paperwork back with her, make herself a sandwich and retire with dignity to her room to work, leaving him to do as he pleased.

So she filled her briefcase and drank the tea Fred gave her and waved him on his way before securing the premises for the night.

All she needed to do was to immerse herself even more deeply than ever in her business, she told herself blithely as she walked down the Cop in the dusky evening light. She need see very little of her husband; he, too, was busy with the new factory premises.

There would certainly be no need for the hours of forced proximity such as they had had to endure in Wales. She was still unable to forgive herself for the way he had made her feel on that first night. And she certainly hadn't forgiven him for the way he had tried it on!

What had made it even worse, in retrospect, had been facing the fact that he didn't even fancy her. She left him cold. He was obviously a highly sexed male animal and, as far as she knew, hadn't enjoyed any female companionship for at least three weeks. And when they'd bumped into each other sheer sexual frustration had taken over. All cats were grey in the dark, or so it was said, and any female body, displayed in slinky satin, would have sufficed. He certainly hadn't gnashed his teeth when she had firmly put him in his place!

Her face felt hot as she reached the bridge and cut off down the lane at the side. But that was down to the brisk walk, she told herself as she leaned over the parapet to watch the swirling grey waters of the Severn, quieting her mind before she went into the house.

There was nothing to fear, of course there wasn't. His behaviour had been faultless for the rest of their stay. He had acted on his own advice and put what had happened right out of his mind. And if he'd noticed her edginess, the tight expression on her pale little face, he had made no comment, dragging her off on long cliff walks, behaving like a big brother, the exercise, his amusing companionship eventually helping her to relax, to forget the threat he posed.

But there was no threat, she reminded herself quickly. He would have taken her to his bed, despite their agreement, if she'd been willing. But only because she had been there and he had been missing the more intimate kind of female companionship. He hadn't been bothered, either way. Recalling how quickly he'd dropped his attempted seduction was proof of that. Nothing bothered him except his business empire. As long as he was in charge of that, forging ahead to new and even dizzier heights, he was not capable of taking anything else seriously.

Not even the loss of a considerable inheritance.

When they had met, by utter chance, he had already been running out of time where his grandfather's stipulations had been concerned. He had known, weeks and weeks before, that in order to inherit he had to marry. He had done absolutely nothing about meeting those requirements. He had probably shrugged those impressive shoulders and written the whole thing off. The loss of a fortune hadn't troubled him one scrap. Probably hadn't even entered his head.

Until they had met.

She wasn't the type to turn him on, but she'd do at a pinch. His devious mind would have latched on to the fact that her marriage would be the only thing to stop Graham's tiresome pursuit of her. Therefore she could be persuaded to enter into a sham of a marriage, just for the sake of peace. She would make no bothersome demands on him and then, when the time was right, they could go their separate ways and he would be wealthier than ever. No bother.

So no, he wasn't a threat.

Honey shivered. She had been standing here for far too long. Most of the light had leached from the sky and the river was black, just a few reflected pin-pricks of light on the swirling surface.

Digging into her bag, she extracted her doorkey with frozen fingers and tramped up the path. The house looked deserted, she thought disconsolately, and wondered why her heart felt more buoyant when light flooded into the tiny hallway from the kitchen at the rear of the house as she opened the door and let herself in.

'And how was your day?'

He was wearing a white shirt, open at the neck, the sleeves rolled back. It contrasted crisply with the healthy bronze of his skin, the thick soft blackness of his hair, the shadow of stubble on his tough jawline. And his narrow hips, the endless leanness of his legs, were encased in hugging dark denim and it was warm in here and a delicious savoury aroma was wafting from the kitchen and, suddenly, the little house felt almost like home.

But it wasn't. It was just a place to live for the time being. After Folly Field she doubted if she'd ever feel truly, spiritually at home in any house. Even her flat, cosy as it had been, had been a very poor second best.

'Oh, fine. And yours?' She was being polite and didn't have to wait for an answer and was halfway up the narrow staircase when his voice bit out,

'You're late. I was on the point of coming to look for you.'

'How quaint.' She retraced two of the steps and thrust her head over the banister, her eyes very cool and determined as they swept the suddenly cold austerity of his face. 'We are not a normal married couple. We are not answerable to each other.' And watched the unforgettable features relax just a little, heard the hateful mockery slide back into his voice as he concurred,

'On that I whole-heartedly agree. However, it might be useful to let one another know. A scribbled note would do. If Avril phoned, or one of my parents, it might be awkward if one or other of us had to admit to not knowing where the other was.'

She withdrew her head and went on up. He had a point. They had barely got here last night before her mother had phoned wanting to know if they had had a lovely time on their honeymoon. Huh! And she had hardly finished her tour of the rooms to check that the removal firm had positioned the things from her former flat in roughly the right places when Ben had put a call through to Fanny to ask how his father was.

He was fine, would be out of hospital in a few days, and would phone to speak to them himself. So yes, a rough idea of where they both were, at what time they could be expected back here, might be a good idea if this deceitful charade were to be maintained.

'Dinner will be on the table in half an hour.' His voice followed her up the stairs. The house was so small there was no need to bellow, and heaven only knew how he thought they were going to entertain more than one thin person!

Suddenly feeling bone-weary, Honey sank down on the top step and her voice was unconsciously plaintive as she let him know, 'You go ahead. I don't want any.' Then blinked as he appeared, as if by magic, at the foot of the stairs. He had a corkscrew in one hand, a wooden spoon in the other but the domestic accessories didn't make him look like a nice tame pussycat. He looked quite alarmingly ferocious.

'Look at you,' he said with cold anger, his eyes glinting beneath the black bar of his lowered brows.

'You are tired, you are dirty. You need a hot shower and a good meal. I intend to see you have both. You look like a street urchin. Now get!'

She got. She knew when to be prudent.

But the street urchin taunt rankled and, the grime of the day washed away beneath the shower, she set out proving him wrong. She had not had time to unpack the suitcases the removal men had brought from her flat but after a quick rummage she found what she wanted.

Just a tracksuit. But beautifully cut in a soft silk velvet. The deep port-wine colour subtly emphasised the pale perfection of her skin, the glowing darkness of her eyes and the vibrant red of her hair. Flamboyant crystal earrings glittered and swung among the riotous curls and the collarless top was left unbuttoned just far enough to reveal the sparkle of a single crystal pendant as it nestled between her breasts.

Scarlet lips were a glossy pout, contrasting startlingly with the whiteness of her skin as, bare-footed, she glided into the kitchen. Street urchin, indeed! She would make him eat his words!

Ben didn't even blink, although she knew she was colourful enough to make any normal man reach for his shades.

'We're eating in the dining-room. Go on through, everything's ready,' he ordered tightly, taking a salad from the fridge. And Honey walked ahead, miffed, not even bothering to swing her hips. He wouldn't notice her if she came wrapped in gold leaf, diamonds stuffed in every known orifice!

If there was just enough room to swing a cat in the kitchen one could swing a medium-sized dog in the dining-room, at a pinch, she thought sourly. And sat down at the table, asking huffily, 'You said you would need to entertain. I can't think how. Did you always have the ambition to live in a shoe box?'

'Eat, and be quiet. It might improve your mood,' he instructed equably, ladling a rich chicken and vegetable casserole from the steaming earthenware pot in the centre of the table that had once graced her flat.

He passed her the plate, helping himself now, and somehow, between grudgingly admitting that he had gone to a great deal of trouble, that the food was good, very good, the bottle of burgundy just to her liking, she began to relax and finally acknowledged, 'Go to the top of the class. I've often wondered what it would be like to have a tame cook in the kitchen—lovely hot meals waiting for me when I finish work.'

'Don't get too used to it.' She thought she detected a rare flash of anger in those uncharted blue eyes, but couldn't be sure. She was too sleepy, too replete to care. She smiled gently at him across the table and didn't stop, not even when he asked, 'Why do you dislike men? I've heard you always hold them at arm's length.'

She shook her head, her big brown eyes drowsing at him as she corrected, 'You make me sound like a rabid feminist. I'm not.'

'Yet apart from the hapless Graham, who doesn't count, I've been told you haven't dated for ages.' He topped up her wine glass, his eyes holding hers steadily. 'You've never been short of offers, but you never take any of them up.'

'True.' She smiled at him dreamily. He was superb to look at. Pity he was such a bastard. Conning his ancient, dying grandfather for the sake of a few extra millions—or whatever. Quite happy to marry a woman he couldn't care for, didn't even see, for the sake of a fatter bank account. But right now she couldn't rake up all that usual ire; she was too content to bother. So she sipped a little more of her wine and expanded, twirling the glass between her fingers, 'I've been too busy setting up my business and getting it up and running to bother looking for the right man. But if and when I find him I'll be perfectly happy to marry and raise a family with him. I am normal, you know,' she tacked on breathily because something about the glint in his eyes warned her she had somehow annoyed him again.

And she knew she had when he reminded her coldly, 'You are already married—to me! And I'd like to point out that that only came about because you wanted to rid yourself of Graham in the most final way possible. And because, equally important, the marriage was not to be consummated. So exactly how normal does that make you?'

There was a point to be made there, somewhere. But she felt far too relaxed and fuddled to figure it out. Taking refuge in defence, she queried right back, 'And who told you about my private life? You've barely been in this area a month and yet you claim to know all about my sex life. Or lack of it.'

'Sonia,' he said without an apparent qualm and Honey hunched her shoulders, frowning down at the tablecloth.

She might have known. Gossip was Sonia's life-blood, Ben would only have had to ask an innocent question for her to supply a million answers, the more titillating the better. She and Honey had been at school together and in latter years Sonia had clung on, making sure the friendship didn't die out altogether. Which meant that her so-called friend knew practically all there was to know about her and wasn't at all averse to passing it on.

Not that there was anything in her life she need be ashamed of, but she hated to think of Ben and Sonia getting together and putting her life under a microscope, and there was already a warning flush of colour on her cheekbones before he said with level persistence, 'It's only a suggestion, but maybe you dislike men in general because none of them lives up to the memory of your father. You and he were extremely close. Or maybe——' he had his forearms on the table now, leaning towards her '—his death, occuring when you were at a particularly vulnerable age, was responsible for your inability to fall in love, making you fear the loss of a loved one, the loss of love, more than you fear being on your own.'

His memorable eyes had never been gentler but Honey's mood of relaxation was shattered. How dared he imply she was incapable of loving? What was she supposed to be? Emotionally barren, or something?

She sprang to her feet, upsetting her chair, glaring at him from furious eyes, her hands planted firmly on her hips.

'Spare me your clumsy attempts at amateur psychology; I don't need them,' she flung at him. 'If you think I've got some kind of deep-seated neurosis you can bloody well think again! I just don't like being pawed around—and members of your sex have been trying to do that since I was in my teens! And I'd rather stay home nights than have to fight to keep my date out of my bed!' Her breasts were heaving dramatically, straining against the soft fabric of her top and she knew she was going to explode, and say things she might possibly regret. And throw things.

She stamped to the door but couldn't resist one final outraged howl. 'And I'm perfectly capable of falling in love—if I ever get lucky enough to meet the right man. Not that it's any business of yours!'

And saw a slow wicked smile enliven his erstwhile studiously expressionless features, heard the low purr of his voice as he tossed right back to her, 'I'm delighted to hear it, my little nest of vipers. And you never know, I just might make it my business.'

What he had meant by that cheap gibe she didn't know. Didn't want to know, either. Honey burrowed deeper into her duvet to block out the sounds of his early morning splashing about in the bathroom.

She had scarcely slept a wink all night for hating him and the last thing she wanted to hear was the evidence that he was still drawing breath!

How dared he suggest that there was something wrong with her, that she was twisted—a suitable case for treatment? Not only had he made it plain that, as far as he was concerned, she was one huge turn-off—and that was bad enough—but he had had the gall to imply she was emotionally warped.

The intensity of her loathing surprised her. She had never hated anyone in her life but was making up for lost time with a vengeance, she decided, ramming her fingers in her ears because the louse was now running down the stairs. Whistling!

And for the next half-hour she would undoubtedly have to endure listening to him clattering around in the kitchen, making his breakfast. Sounds carried in this tiny house; you couldn't get away from them. And of course he wouldn't have wanted to buy something larger, where there was room to move around without falling over each other. Mr Big-Shot had gone out and rented the smallest and possibly cheapest pad he could find. He wouldn't be in the area for long, and they wouldn't need to stay married for long. So he wouldn't waste his money.

Crossly, she poked her rumpled head out of the duvet and yes, sure enough, she could hear him in the kitchen. She sat up against the pillows, her arms crossed high over her chest. If he carried breakfast up to her he would find himself carrying it down again. All over his head!

But he didn't come near her and when she finally heard the front door close behind him she felt inexplicably let down and strangely lonely. Which was, she recognised, rather stupid of her. But her temper did tend to die as quickly as it flared to life and the aftermath could be this feeling of emptiness.

It was time she was getting ready for work herself and she tiredly forced herself to get moving. A quick cup of coffee was all she needed and she was just pouring water over granules when the wall-mounted phone in the kitchen rang out.

Probably her mother, wanting to meet her for lunch, she guessed unenthusiastically. It would be difficult to pretend to be a besotted bride when she was anything but, and Avril was a difficult lady to fool.

Sighing, she reached for the instrument and gave the number, her tone resigned, and an unknown masculine voice barked, 'Who is that?'

'Honey—er—Claremont,' she gave the married name she didn't think she would ever get used to, thankful for the reprieve, although she knew she wouldn't be able to avoid Avril for long. She suggested, 'You've probably got the wrong number.'

'I've got no such thing!'

Honey held the receiver further away from her ear. Whoever he was, he had got out of the wrong side of the bed this morning. And then her eyes went very wide as the voice positively growled down the line.

'You're the woman who married my grandson. Is Ben around?'

'Oh!' Honey tried to grapple her thoughts in order. He didn't sound like an ill old man, and certainly not like a man who was expected to breathe his last at any moment.

'Did you say no? Speak up, woman!'

She hadn't, but she'd meant to. Ben hadn't said his grandfather was a grouch. But then, any man who would put such a condition in his will just had to be unpleasant.

'Ben's already left for work,' she answered coolly. 'Shall I ask him to call you when he gets back?'

'And when will that be, may I ask?'

The old boy's mood wasn't improving, Honey thought with a glint in her eye. And, on his last legs or not, she would tell him to mind his manners if he didn't cool it. Reaching for the sheet of paper Ben had left on the table, she quickly scanned the bold, decisive scrawl and told him icily, 'Not until late. He has a business dinner.'

'At least some things don't change.' Oddly enough, he sounded mollified. 'When he does find time, tell him to phone. I have a bone to pick with the young scoundrel. Why wasn't I invited to your wedding?'

'Would you have come?' Honey didn't know what else to say. And, ill as he was supposed to be, could he have come?'

'Like a shot! If only to make sure he knew what he was doing. Ben's got a cool head on his shoulders; he knew what he wanted and he went out and got it. Marriage doesn't mix with big business. I should know. Had four of 'em myself. All disasters! Except for the second—and that was only saved from total failure when Ben's father was born. Got nothing whatsoever out of the other three!'

'How astonishing.' There was a cold bite beneath her deliberately sugar-sweet tone, a bite that deepened as she tacked on, 'Four failed marriages—and you such a gentle old sweetie.'

She fully expected him to slam the receiver down, and didn't much care if he did. But he gave a grudging snort of laughter and told her, 'You're obviously a bit of an acid-drop yourself. Now, you tell that husband of yours to get you out here. I want to take a good look at you. And if I suspect, for one second, that you married my grandson for his money then he's out of my will for a start. Out! You might get your hands on what he's worked for, but you won't see a penny of any money of mine!'

'And you have a nice day, too!' Honey muttered under her breath as the line went dead. But, far from angering her, the old man had intrigued her. The irascible old devil was obviously fighting fit and he was so anti-marriage it wasn't true!

Ben had lied when he'd told her that his sick old grandfather would disinherit him if he didn't marry and settle down within the time stipulated.

Why?

Just what was Ben Claremont up to?

CHAPTER SIX

FOR the first time ever Honey's thoughts were not on her work and she was still chewing over the ramifications of what she had learned when she walked slowly back to the house by the river that evening.

Ben had lied about his reasons for needing to marry. Her conversation—if it could be called that—with his grandfather had made that much clear. Far from threatening to disinherit his only grandchild if he failed to marry before the end of the stipulated period, he was threatening to do exactly that if she, Honey, didn't meet with his approval! Obviously, the old man didn't hold the married state in much esteem and wasn't at all happy to learn that Ben had allowed himself to be trapped!

So the question was, why had Ben lied?

She wouldn't know until she asked.

And he, according to the note he'd left, wouldn't be in until later. The hours stretched before her and she wrinkled her nose in self-disgust. Impatience wouldn't make the time pass more quickly so she changed into jeans and an old sweatshirt, made herself a salad then began unpacking the clothes which were still in suitcases, and re-positioning the things that had been brought from her flat to her own liking.

At eleven o'clock she went up for a shower then padded downstairs in her robe, towelling her hair as she went. The business dinner couldn't last much longer, surely? He would be home soon. In fact she'd expected him ages ago. And the inner bubble of excitement had nothing to do with any eagerness to be in his company, she assured herself staunchly; she was simply anxious to know why he had lied.

He had had some other reason for wanting to marry her. The disinheritance statement didn't hold water and she was going to demand the truth.

But at least that revealing conversation with his grandfather had completely overshadowed all the resentment she'd felt when he'd as good as accused her of being emotionally barren, she acknowledged as she curled up in an armchair to wait. Maybe, one day, she would tell him the whole truth, tell him how her reservations about the opposite sex had begun . . .

'Waiting up for me, Honey? Can I dare to hope you're turning into a dutiful wife?'

The rich drawly voice sent a shattering skitter of shivers all the way down her spine and she ignored the sudden twist of pleasure that came from looking at six-feet-something of lean manhood clad in a superbly cut formal dark suit, looked pointedly at her watch and snapped, 'You must have had a fascinating dinner companion. It's almost midnight.'

His long mouth curled with amusement. 'I hoped in vain, obviously.' He moved further into the room, closing the door behind him. 'Never mind. The tired business executive will fix a drink for his wife. This one's not afraid of a little role reversal. Gin? Whisky?'

'Anything.' She wriggled round on her knees, watching him over the back of the armchair as he walked over to the drinks table and poured Scotch into two glasses. He didn't look in the least tired. If anything, she was sure she could detect a kind of simmering excitement beneath all that suavely assured composure. Had tonight's dinner been purely a business thing?

He turned then and his lancing blue eyes met hers and held. Honey felt herself go pink and slithered back down the chair, reorganising herself into the seat with the feeling she'd been caught doing something she shouldn't. Like looking at her husband.

Her gyrations had made the edges of her robe fly open, revealing practically all there was to reveal. And she just knew her face was as red as her hair as he stood over her, nursing the drinks, waiting while she tugged the slithery silk modestly back into place. And his face was bored.

Even if he did rate the sight of her semi-nakedness about as exciting as reading the telephone directory from cover to cover, he didn't have to make it so obvious, did he? she fumed as she stiffly accepted the glass he gave her. And did he think she'd deliberately allowed her robe to fall open as a prelude to something else?

The very idea both humiliated and enraged her and she bit out, not thinking, 'So who were you with tonight?' Which made her sound like a jealous wife and to show she regretted the unguarded question she tagged on, 'Not that I'm interested, of course. But you are rather late—for a boring business dinner.'

'It was far from boring, I assure you.' He put his glass on the mantelpiece and shed his suit jacket, tossing it on to the table. His tie followed. 'We went to the Rainbow Fleece. You know it, of course?'

'Certainly.' She felt her face muscles stiffen. The restaurant, a few miles out in the country, was the last word in elegance, shockingly expensive. She had been there once, as Henry's guest—with Avril and Graham, naturally. Henry had had the occasion earmarked as a celebration. On the way over, travelling in separate cars, Graham had proposed for the first time—probably because Henry had told him it was high time they got the thing settled. And, at that stage, Henry had been quite confident that no woman alive would fail to grab Graham's offer with cries of glee!

Honey had enjoyed the superb food and the excellent service but Henry had become increasingly angry when no engagement announcement had been forthcoming and Graham had looked like a whipped dog. So she would have liked to dine there again, in less fraught circumstances, and lap up the atmosphere of exclusivity.

And Ben had been there all evening, having a 'far from boring' time, while she had been here, shifting furniture and unpacking suitcases, nibbling unenthusiastically at an uninspired salad.

He had opened the collar of his shirt and kicked off his shoes and now he stretched out on the sofa, a cushion behind his head, sipping his drink with his eyes half closed. Totally relaxed, while she was getting more strung up by the moment.

'And you didn't have to wait up, you know. You mustn't, in future. When one is really enjoying oneself time slips by unnoticed, don't you find?' His sleepy, speedwell-blue eyes shifted to hers, that enigmatic, secret smile curling the corners of his mouth. 'You can go to bed now, now I'm safely gathered in.'

Honey pulled in a deep breath, holding in the explosion. So he wasn't going to tell her who he'd been with, whose company had been enjoyable enough to make time slip by unnoticed. And she couldn't ask again because she'd already told him she didn't want to know. And he'd as good as said that this evening's dinner engagement was only the first of many, and he'd implied that she'd waited up for him like an anxious wife.

But she was going to have to grow up around him, rein in her regrettably explosive temper, if she were to best him. And best him she would!

So her voice was beautifully calm, as if she were merely discussing the weather, when she informed him, 'Your grandfather dragged himself off his deathbed this morning to phone you. You'd already left, of course, but we had a very interesting conversation.' And watched his body go very still, and smiled to herself because two could play the patronising game.

'And what did he have to say for himself?' He sounded only slightly interested, which meant, Honey knew, that he had quickly combatted whatever it was that had made him tense up. Taking his time, he swallowed the last of his drink and swung his feet to the floor, his head tipped on one side in idle query.

She told him, 'Quite a lot, and most of it loudly. Certainly enough to leave me in no doubt that, far from wanting you to marry, he's dead against it. You lied to me. Why?'

'Ah.'

The warm slide of his eyes over her stern little face made her pulses flutter alarmingly. But she wouldn't let him make her angry again, she wouldn't, and her pointed chin went fractionally higher.

He got smoothly to his feet, completely unfazed as he confided, 'It was only a matter of time before the lie was discovered. I knew that, of course.' He put his empty glass on the table and held out a hand for hers, took it, and placed it beside his. 'We'll deal with these in the morning. Time for bed now, it's late. Coming up?'

Whether she was or not, he was halfway to the door when she gathered herself together, jumped to her feet and demanded, 'You didn't want to marry to safeguard an inheritance—so tell me the real reason. What did you expect to gain? I think I deserve to know!'

'Do you?' He reached for his discarded suit jacket and hooked it over his shoulder and walked to the door. 'Maybe I wanted a little nest of vipers to call my own.'

His parting smile was bland enough to make her ache to bounce right over and slap him. But she restrained herself. One day she would force him to·

tell the truth, discover what he had expected to gain by entering into this loveless marriage. Or she would die in the attempt!

It was a strange game they were playing, she admitted to herself a fortnight later. There had been no more business dinners, lengthy or otherwise, and Ben had stopped patronising her. And she, in turn, seemed to have got her volatile temper under control. At least, he didn't say or do anything to annoy her any more. Though whether by design or accident she didn't know.

Whoever returned first in the evenings made the meal and afterwards, if the weather was fine, they walked by the river or drove into the countryside. If it was wet or chilly Ben lit a fire and they listened to Honey's catholic selection of tapes. And talked. They always seemed to be talking and if they disagreed on a subject they didn't fight about it. Which was nice. He had somehow become her friend, Honey thought with a warm glow. Her best friend, quite probably.

Ben had few possessions; all the furniture, the pictures, linen and knick-knacks were Honey's, brought from her flat, and when she commented on the fact that all he seemed to own was his clothes he merely shrugged, giving her that wonderful, melting smile.

'I travel light. It's easier to move on if you don't have to haul packing cases around with you.'

'Sensible,' Honey agreed with an approving smile which successfully masked the sudden anguish of her thoughts. When the time was right, for both of them, their paper marriage would be over, she knew that; it was part of the bargain. Ben would only need to pack a suitcase, collect his briefcase, and leave. It would probably take about ten minutes, if that.

But it wouldn't be yet, she thought, unwilling to question why she should immediately feel more cheerful. She hadn't seen Henry or Graham since her marriage but her mother would have told her if Graham had started to date someone else.

And she still didn't know the real reason behind Ben's need to marry so she had no way of knowing when the time would be right for him to call it a day. And she wasn't going to ask. She was deeply reluctant to start another fight. Not that he had ever been really angry with her, she recognised; the rage had all been on her side.

Shrugging out of her introspective mood, she began to stack the supper dishes.

'Why don't we redecorate? We could make this place so much more like home if we got rid of all the ghastly wallpaper.' The rented property had been newly decorated when they'd moved in but the overpowering wallpaper combined with the ugly shade of pale puce used for the paintwork was definitely not to Honey's taste and Ben had admitted it was all a florid nightmare. 'It's Sunday tomorrow so we could make a start. Strip the walls. And we could meet up on Monday, at lunchtime, and pick out something we could both live with.'

'Sorry, tomorrow's out, I'll be knee-deep in paperwork.' He helped her carry the debris of their meal through to the kitchen. 'I'm flying out to New

York on Monday for a meeting with my board of directors. There are a few things I need to iron out, Stateside, and then I'll be tied up at the London head office for a couple of days. I don't think I'll get back in much under a week.'

He was stacking the dishwasher and he suddenly seemed distant, as if he were already moving away. Out of her life.

'You didn't tell me. Would you have said anything if I hadn't talked about stripping the walls tomorrow?' Her voice was panicky, and she didn't know why. 'Or would you have simply left me a note?'

'You sound as if you don't want me to go.' He straightened up, his eyes mocking. 'Shall you miss me?'

Miss him? Would she? Had she given herself away? Was there anything to give away, in any case? Was there? Hating the sudden confusion of her thoughts, she got to grips with them and pushed them into limbo, making her voice buoyant, her smile very wide and bright.

'I'll miss having you around to help with the chores so I guess I'll just get out and socialise more. Talking of socialising——' she knew she was putting on an act but couldn't figure out why she needed to '—we haven't done any. People expect it. So why don't I organise a small dinner party for when you come back? Just Mother and Sonia and Colin—there isn't room for any more. And why don't I make a start on the redecorating tomorrow?' She was being frightfully busy, tidying the kitchen. Very bright and bubbly. 'If you'll leave the choice of colour schemes to me I could get part of the place done over while you're away.'

'There's no point.' He sounded bored. He looked bored, too. And she hadn't seen that look on his face for a couple of weeks, not since the night she'd told him she knew he'd lied about the reasons behind his need to marry. 'It's not a home, is it? It's simply a place to stay. We won't be here for long enough to merit the trouble.'

The feeling of depression lingered on into the middle of the following week. Honey tried to put it down to having to live with the hideous colour schemes, the garish floral wallpaper, but knew she was lying to herself.

Ben had been right, of course. They wouldn't be living here together for long enough to justify the extra work and expense of redecorating. And although she could have done out the main living rooms herself, paying for the materials out of her own pocket, she couldn't seem to summon the energy or enthusiasm.

Why should she, when Ben didn't care what their surroundings were? As he had pointed out, this place wasn't home. And that mattered to her.

And now she was missing him.

But she mustn't, she told herself as she wrapped a pair of Georgian wine glasses in masses of tissue and carefully placed them into a box for a satisfied customer. Because although they had become friends, warm companions, she mustn't let him become part of her life. He certainly didn't intend to get closer to her than necessary. He hadn't even phoned to let her know he'd arrived safely in New York.

The customer departed and there was no one left. Honey dragged her fingers through her hair and heaved a sigh. Fred was busy in the workshop and she'd been frantically dealing with customers all morning until now, and the amount she had taken should have left her feeling buoyant and she would be meeting Nick Devlin for lunch in half an hour in the spit-and-sawdust pub down the road.

But even the possibility that Nick might have something really outstanding to offer her didn't raise her spirits. So it was high time, she instructed herself firmly, she did something about it. It was pointless to let herself become dependent on Ben. They wouldn't be together long, and when he had gone she would be alone again, and would enjoy being her own woman, just as she had before. She had not been dependent on another human being since her father died and wasn't going to start now.

In the middle of her productive self-lecturing session Nick Devlin phoned.

'The van packed up on me; it's being fixed now. I don't know how long it'll take, but we should be able to meet up this evening. I've got a couple of pewter spoons—fifteenth century, at a guess, diamond-point knops—and a Charles the First flagon you'd kill for. Plus the usual crop of Pilgrim badges and rings. So I'll see you at the usual place some time between six and seven. Unless you'd rather I met you at your flat?'

'I'm not in the flat any more,' she told him quickly, thinking fast. She didn't want to hang around waiting in the pub and she certainly didn't want to miss the opportunity of having first refusal of his latest harvest from the Thames. If she didn't agree to see him this evening he would carry on straight up to Chester then Liverpool to the other dealers who regularly bought from him.

Giving directions to the house on the riverside, she added, 'There's plenty of parking space at the end of the terrace; I'll be there after six. And don't bother to stop for a meal on the way; I'll feed you.'

Knowing his predilection for pub food—on which he seemed to exist, as far as she could gather—she picked up a pizza on the way home and a pack of canned beer and let herself into the empty house.

It had been a warm day and the place felt stuffy. She went to change, flinging windows open on the way. She was going to take charge of her own life again from now on. Her self-lecture had had the desired effect and one of the first things she must do was decide where she would live when her sham of a marriage was over. She definitely wouldn't go back to live above the shop. Already the extra display space was reaping benefits she would be a fool to ignore.

There was no reason why she shouldn't stay on here, she decided, hanging up the cream linen suit she had worn all day and stepping into a brief pair of plum-coloured shorts, topping them with a loose oyster silk sleeveless blouse, the ends tied loosely around her midriff.

Barefooted, she padded downstairs, pondering. Although the house was small it was pretty and quite adequate for one, close enough to her business with the added bonus of being off the main road with the ever-changing waters of the Severn gliding beneath her windows. And if she were to stay here she could go ahead with the redecorating, no matter what Ben had decided. It would be nothing to do with him. She would tell him of her decision when she saw him next.

If she ever did. He might already have grown tired of playing at marriage, or his reason for entering into it in the first place might no longer be valid. And she had no time to examine the pang produced by that particular scenario because the hammering on the door told her that Nick had arrived.

'You promised to feed me,' was his greeting, and Honey opened the door wider, her eyes fixed avidly on the large cardboard box he was clutching to his leather-clad chest. 'Dinky place, scary wallpaper.' He walked on through and Honey grinned at his back. In all the years she had known him he hadn't changed. In his late twenties now, she guessed, he still looked like a tearaway. Black leather everything, lank dark hair tied back in a pigtail, designer stubble and laughing amber eyes. If he were a pop star he would be idolised.

'So you got the van fixed, finally?' Honey asked drily as he sank down on the sofa, using the box as a footstool. It was already well past seven. She was more than glad she hadn't agreed to wait for him in the pub.

'Sort of.' He didn't seem much interested. 'The cowing heap's ready for the scrap-yard. And you can forget the goodies. You can look while I eat.'

No point in arguing. Honey went contentedly enough to the kitchen and popped the lavishly topped pizza in the oven, put a plate and a knife on a tray, took his beer through and poured herself a glass of wine. She was itching to see what he had brought and the sooner his food was ready, the sooner she'd be able to look.

They had made contact at an antiques fair three years ago. He had hovered, watching while she had haggled over a pewter dish and had later sidled up, asking if she was interested in early pewter, offering to show her what he had in the back of his van.

Swallowing her misgivings, she had gone with him and had congratulated herself ever afterwards for taking that calculated risk. Nick Devlin was a licensed beachcomber, one of the tight-knit group of 'mudlarks' who picked over jealously guarded stretches of the Thames's tidal foreshore, going out with metal detectors after every tide and every storm, picking over the spoil heaps from building sites near the historic river.

And three or four times a year they met on his way up north and she always had the pick of his haul to sell on in her shop. And because of that he was special to her, even though they knew little more about each other than name and occupation. On the whole, she thought as she carried his tray through, a highly satisfactory way to conduct business.

He had already downed a couple of cans and as she gave him the tray with the bubbling pizza and a bowl of oven chips he took his feet from the box and pushed it towards her. And it was two hours later when Honey fished her cheque-book from her bag and tapped the end of her pen against her teeth.

'I'm not sure about the flagon. It's pricey.'

Nick shrugged, taking the top off the last can of beer. 'Take it or leave it. You'll sell it on for double that.'

'I know. But it could take months. It's a lot to be tied up.' Yet the flagon was beautiful, tall and elegant, perfect, right down to the bun lid, the knop and thumbpiece intact. Just a minor dent on one side, which Fred could tease out.

'It should be in a museum.' Nick wiped his mouth with the back of his hand and swung his booted feet up on the sofa. 'You won't get the chance of anything like it, not in your lifetime. Tell you what, take it and I'll throw in the rest of the stuff. You've earmarked the pick and it will save me the drive up north. Doubt if the van would make it up and back down south again, in any case.' And Honey was lost.

Quickly, before she could change her mind, she added the cost of the flagon to the other items she was buying and wrote the cheque.

'You won't regret it.' Nick rolled off the sofa and put the cheque in the back pocket of his tight leather trousers and Honey asked, thinking of all that beer, 'Where are you staying tonight?' She would feel guilty if he were to head back to London. She had supplied the alcohol that would take him over the legal limit.

'You offering, or something?' Amber eyes ate up
the long shapely legs left bare by the brief shorts
and Honey went rigid.

'Definitely not! But I could phone round and find
you a bed and breakfast place. It's not too late.'

'Just teasing—not testing.' His eyes laughed into
hers, coaxing a smile. 'I know better than to mix
business with pleasure. And it would be a pleasure,
believe me! No, princess,' he tacked on hurriedly
as she primmed her mouth and wished she'd worn
something smothering, 'I'd be a fool to spoil a good
deal, wouldn't I? Besides, I've got a lovely live-in
lady. I never did get round to telling you about
Clara, did I? Some other time, maybe. And don't
worry, I always carry my bedroll in the back of the
van. Now——' he touched the carefully repacked
box of pewter with the scuffed toe of his boot
'—where do you want this lot? Got a safe here?'

She shook her head. The flagon, in particular,
should be somewhere safe for the night, and she
suggested, 'The wardrobe in my room has a lock
and a key. If I sleep with the key under my pillow
I'd hear if someone broke in and tried to force the
door.' Not that she thought anyone would, but
better be safe than the other. Nick picked up the
box.

'Lead the way, princess. It's a fair weight.'

With the box and its precious contents safely
stowed in the wardrobe, the door locked and the
key under her pillow, Honey led the way out of the
room, telling him, 'As always, it's been a pleasure.
But next time try not to put quite so much temptation in my way!' She smiled at him over her

shoulder, wondering at his puzzled frown. 'You know I can't resist. Trouble is, you know my weaknesses far too well!'

She turned to follow the direction of his frowning eyes. And froze.

'Ben!'

She hadn't heard his key in the door, or heard him mount the stairs. Just seeing him there, so dark, so tall, so utterly splendid, was making her heart flop around inside her chest, and she knew she was babbling, but couldn't help it as she told him, 'You should have let me know. I didn't expect you home so soon!'

If she'd known, she would have made sure her business with Nick had been completed ages ago, would have made sure she had a good meal ready to be served, a proper welcome, because she now knew——

'That much is patently obvious.' His voice was grim, his face stark. He stood aside at the head of the stairs and said tightly, 'Out, you, whoever you are. Now.' And then, as Nick squared his shoulders, frowning across at Honey, Ben repeated, 'Now. Unless you like being plastered across the wall.'

And as Nick showed no inclination to move Honey gulped down the lump of horror in her throat and babbled,

'You haven't met my husband, Nick. Ben, this is Nick Devlin, my——'

'Don't say it!' Ben grated, and Nick's eyebrows shot up to his hairline. Turning to Honey, his shoulders lifting, his hands spread wide, he told her, 'I'll split, then. See you around, princess.' And sped lightly down the stairs as if the sleight of foot needed to escape from irate husbands had been programmed into him at birth.

Honey didn't see him go. The only thing occupying her whirling mind was Ben's face. Every taut line was a savage indictment. He looked as if he would like to kill her and his blue eyes raked scathingly over her face before he marched into her bedroom.

She knew what he was thinking and why he was thinking it and, after a breathless pause, she scurried after him.

'So you tidied away the evidence.' He gestured savagely at the demure, unrumpled bed. 'Or couldn't you wait to get between the sheets? Did he take you on the floor?'

'You crude bastard!' Incensed, Honey planted her hands on her curvy hips, her dark eyes spitting knives. What right had he to believe that of her? To condemn her without a hearing?

'Well, did he?' he demanded raspingly, his eyes narrowed to blazing sapphire slits, his hands clamping on her shoulders as if he was about to shake the life out of her.

'What's it to do with you?' she yelled, beside herself with rage.

How could he think such things of her? She tried to shrug his hands away but didn't succeed and she wanted to hurt him as much as his crude accusation had hurt her, wanted to give him something to really get in a rage about.

She would have liked to tell him, 'Yes, on the floor—and on the kitchen table, and then in the bath, not forgetting on the riverbank in full view of every passer-by', but didn't quite dare and contented herself with spitting out, 'We had a bargain, remember? An open marriage, as long as we were discreet.'

He went very still, his hands tightening on her shoulders, his eyes lancing into hers. She wondered wildly if he was going to strangle her, but he said tightly, his lips barely moving, 'I've just rewritten the rules. If that creep ever comes near you again I'll kill him.'

'Tough guy!' she taunted heatedly, too angry herself now to judge how far she could go before his control snapped. 'When I tell him he'll shake in his shoes!'

Then she wished she'd held her tongue because she had never seen such stark, murderous rage before and this wasn't the man she had come to look on as her friend, the man she had pined for, and he made that very clear as he dragged her hard against his body, his steel-hard arms pinioning her as he blazed, 'When I've finished with you, you'll never want to see another man again, let alone that leather-clad, pigtailed jerk!'

CHAPTER SEVEN

THE assault of Ben's mouth on hers nearly shocked the life out of Honey, the punishment almost too much to take. Because it was white-hot conflagration—her body was going up in flames, burning.

The cleaving of body to heated body, of mouth to passionate, ravaging mouth was elemental, basic and undeniable, and Honey recognised the wild shudders of uncontrol that shook his frame because they exactly matched her own.

Ben, who had always been so cool, so much in control, was now shaking with passion and she would never have believed it possible, never believed her own emotions could rage in such lost, wild abandon.

His breathing was ragged as he tore his lips from hers, only to replace them after a deep shuddering breath, tenderly tasting her now, taking the sweetness she offered so willingly, her hands clinging to the warm nape of his neck, dragging his head down to hers as she explored his mouth with lavish enjoyment.

And her name was a low moan of need on his lips as his mouth at last followed where his impatient hands had ripped the flimsy blouse from her body, and as he found and suckled the aroused peak of one yearning breast and then the other she went boneless, unprepared for the exquisitely shattering pleasure.

Helplessly, she clung to him, her legs no longer capable of holding her upright. She knew now what she should have realised weeks ago. She loved him. And she had probably been aware of it, on some deep level of consciousness, right from the start. It would explain why she had agreed to marry him. Wanting to rid herself of Graham had had very little to do with it!

Several times over the past few days she had been on the verge of admitting it, she could see that now. And he had been jealous of Nick—and that had to say something about his feelings for her—and he could never again tell her she didn't turn him on!

His dark head at the full bounty of her breasts had her mewing in ecstasy. It was almost more pleasure than she could bear and yet she wanted more. And he was tasting, suckling, nipping with strong white teeth, his breath rasping as if he couldn't get enough of her, and he judged the moment when she could no longer stand, even within the support of his arms, for he scooped her up and put her on the bed, dragging off his suit jacket then sliding away her shorts, taking her tiny briefs along with them.

There was a kind of frenzied patience about the way he dealt with his shirt buttons and she couldn't wait, lifting her arms to him, winding them around his wide shoulders, opening her mouth to tell him she loved him but giving in to the temptation to kiss him instead.

It was beautiful. Wonderful. So very special. Words could come later, much, much later. And the world began to spin around her, whisking away the last shreds of her control as his hard body followed the arching, inviting curve of hers down on to the bed, covering her, one of his hands gliding between her thighs.

'Ben...' Tiny moans of ecstasy escaped her parted lips. She wanted him so. She would love him all her life. And then she felt the sudden stillness above her and opened her eyes in shock as he rolled off the bed, his movements harsh with suppressed violence.

The lines of his face were frightening in their austere male beauty as he said bitterly, 'You disgust me. Still hot from being bedded by your lover—and my God, he must be the best kept secret in town!—you'd lie on your back for me. Me, or anyone?' He scooped his jacket from the floor. 'But if it's any comfort to you, I disgust myself even more.'

In shock, Honey stared at the blank face of the door he had slammed behind him, her mouth trembling. The warm and beautiful world was now cold and ugly and it was difficult to grasp. But when she did her mind felt as if it would explode with anger.

How dared he think such things of her? How dared he speak to her that way? He had concluded, in his usual know-it-all fashion, that her fastidiousness where sex was concerned was merely a front to hide her degraded need to take secret lovers—the more the merrier!

She hated him! Like a silly, gullible girl, she'd actually thought he'd been jealous of Nick, that he really cared for her, that his lovemaking had been born out of a need to claim her, make her his own. When all it had been was the typical male's base reaction to an available and willing high-class tart!

Stuffing her fist into her mouth to stop herself screaming in temper, she fought the instinct to storm out after him and tell him how wrong he was.

Let him think what he liked. He was hateful! He had been manipulating her, playing on her feelings, ever since they had met. Oh, how she cursed the day! Steadily and surely he had been eroding her spirit, her fiery independence, making her believe she actually needed him!

She neither wanted nor needed him in her life. She had managed perfectly before she had become his paper wife and she could do so again. Just see if she couldn't!

Punching the pillow, she curled up under the duvet. From now on she would arrange her future with calm self-assurance. Never again would she boil and bubble at the first sign of trouble, nor rush full-tilt ahead at the mere whiff of a confrontation. In future, she would be coolly, smoothly determined—especially within her dealings with Ben.

She was, she informed herself staunchly, a changed woman.

She was still angry in the morning, but it was a cold anger, fully contained. She was due at an auction in a neighbouring town at ten and she went downstairs wearing a neat grey cotton skirt and a matching blouse topped by a lightweight scarlet jacket.

The pewter she'd bought from Nick could stay safely locked away until she returned. Then she'd load it in the back of her car and take it to the shop to be priced and displayed. Still wondering if she'd been wise to buy the flagon and hoping she'd be able to sell it on in the very near future, she made for the kitchen and the necessary cup of coffee.

But the unexpected sight of Ben as he sat at the table, papers spread out around him, wearing washed-out jeans and an open-necked black shirt with the sleeves rolled up above his elbows, made her heart contract alarmingly, threatening all that new resolve.

Made of sterner stuff, however, she was able to ignore all the brooding sexiness he seemed to exude without being aware of it and, as his head came up, she looked away, marching to pick up the kettle with her head in the air.

'Before I left you said you'd do some socialising. I didn't realise what you had in mind. Otherwise I wouldn't have been in such a hurry to get back.'

The harshness of the night before was still in his voice and it sent shivers scurrying down Honey's spine. But she returned, quite steadily, above the gush of water as she filled the electric kettle, 'Leave it. There's no point in discussing it. You've already done enough damage.' More than enough, and if he wanted coffee he could make it himself. And when hers was ready she would drink it in the living-room. She didn't want to be anywhere near him.

But Ben had no intention of leaving it. She heard the scrape of his chair as he pushed it back and got to his feet and the hairs on the back of her neck stood on end.

'And what's that supposed to mean?' he wanted to know, his voice smooth and deadly now. And close. Much too close.

'Nick will probably never speak to me again,' she informed him coldly, but her hand was shaking with the effort to keep a check on her temper as she spooned coffee granules into the single mug she had put out on the work surface. 'Your insane bully-boy behaviour has almost certainly ruined a good relationship.'

'Oh, how my heart bleeds!'

It was just too much! No longer able to control her temper, she twisted round on her heels and met the derisory blue of his eyes with a furious glare. Sarcastic swine!

'And how would you like it if I meddled in your business and ruined your contact with a supplier? Nick won't bother to offer me anything ever again if he thinks you're about to leap out of the woodwork and threaten to knock his teeth down his throat!'

She quickly turned her back on him. She wouldn't mention the hurt he'd inflicted when he'd as good as called her a tart, when he'd brought her to the point of wanting to give him everything she had to give and then stalked away, telling her she disgusted him! That particular damage was something she was having to repair all on her own.

Slopping boiling water into the mug, she grabbed
it, went to storm out and cannoned straight into
the unmovable wall of his body. The mug described
a graceful arch in the air, spilling the contents all
over the floor and Honey yelled, 'Now see what
you've made me do!' and pushed past him, fury
making her body shake.

An inescapable hand on her arm stopped her
flight and his voice was curiously soft as he demanded, 'Say that again.'

'Why?' she asked through her teeth. 'You can
see the mess for yourself! Or are you blind, as well
as insane?'

She glared at him through temper-slitted eyes and
saw his mouth curve in a lop-sided, self-denigrating
smile.

'Insanely jealous, perhaps.' His grasp gentled, as
if he knew the fight had so suddenly gone out of
her. And it had. Jealous? Ben? A dangerous
softness was stealing all over her, and her huge
brown eyes were puzzled as he prompted softly,
'Explain what you meant about that young
tearaway being a business contact, Honey. Tell me
what he was doing in your bedroom. Tell me what
you meant when you talked about temptation, the
way he knew your weaknesses, your inability to
resist him.'

The steel in his voice was no longer a threat.
Honey flicked her tongue over her dry lips and
gulped nervously as she watched his hooded eyes
follow the movement. She was letting him get
through to her again. Surely she had learned her
lesson? She would not go all soft and gooey just

because he had said what he had about jealousy. She wasn't that big a fool.

Dragging a deep breath through her nostrils, she flicked his hand away from her arm and told everything there was to tell about her purely business relationship with Nick Devlin, ending coolly, 'I always had first refusal of anything he took up north. And after last night I don't suppose I'll see him again.'

'Honey—what can I say? I'm devastated.'

But he didn't look devastated, she derided silently. He looked like a man who had got his own way. Triumphant. But, at her coldly slicing glance, he said quietly, 'I'm sorry. I thought—but you know what I thought. Look, why don't you give me the guy's number and let me phone and apologise?'

'I don't know it,' she responded dully. 'He always contacted me when he knew he was making the trip up north.'

She stepped over the mess on the floor, avoiding his eyes and he asked sharply, 'Where are you going?'

'There's an auction in Bridgnorth at ten.'

'I'll drive you.' No-nonsense hands put her firmly into the chair he'd been using. 'You're still understandably upset. And there's time for that coffee.'

Fatalistically, she watched as he made the drinks and cleared up the mess. Was he trying to make amends? She didn't know and wouldn't let herself care. All that stinging anger had gone now, and she'd successfully quashed all the damaging softness that had crept stealthily over her when he'd pretended he'd been jealous of Nick Devlin. Never again would she allow him to touch her emotions. Once bitten, twice shy—wasn't that what people said? And all that was left, right at this moment, was a strange apathy, a debilitating sense of emptiness.

'I've booked a table at the Rainbow Fleece,' Ben told her as she locked the shop for the night. He had been at her side all day but she had been functioning like a zombie and had scarcely noticed.

She put the keys in her handbag and answered flatly, 'Enjoy your meal.' And walked quickly along the Shut. As if she could leave him behind. But she couldn't, of course, and he was firmly at her side when he drawled,

'We'll both enjoy it. We'll go home and shower and change and make a night of it.'

'No, thanks.' Her stride increasing majestically, she caught her spindly heel between the cobblestones and his arm snaked around her body, steadying her. She was so shaken by the shattering effect of the brief contact that she couldn't even answer when he overrode her refusal, as if it had never been made.

'We both need to relax. We need to talk, level with each other. And then we can start over, make a new beginning.'

Why? she thought moodily, moderating her pace now, careful not to send herself flying into his arms again. Any levelling would all need to come from him. The reasons behind the way he had lied about his need to marry, and quickly, had to be highly dubious. She didn't want to hear them. She wasn't interested.

So there wasn't anything to talk about, was there? And as for making a new beginning—that she should be so crazy! It would be giving him the go-ahead to manipulate her all over again, to torment her, to leap on her if he felt the urge, wind her up, and then stalk away with that look of disgust on his face—as if he had handled dirt.

So she would shut herself in her room and refuse to go anywhere with him. He could take himself out and she hoped he had a lovely time!

Stomping up the stairs, she refused his invitation to use the bathroom first and shut herself in her room. But, listening to him splashing about, she changed her mind. She would go out. Why not? She needn't be nice to him—but she wouldn't be nasty, either. She would lay down a few very firm guidelines for their future, no matter how short it was likely to be.

The Rainbow Fleece was quite as elegant as she remembered it, even more so, and Honey was thankful she had discarded her earlier intention of wearing just any old thing—just to show him how unimportant to her the evening was—as being too childish to contemplate.

The gold tissue sheath was the most glamorous thing she owned, the short tight skirt flattering her long shapely legs, the clinging top appearing to stay up by will-power alone. A perfect foil for Ben's suavely clad, sensational physique and, even though she positively hated him, she had to admit that he was the most spectacularly attractive man within the radius of a thousand miles. And then some.

And the eyes of other women watched them. There was some malice for her own flamboyance, Honey recognised, but a heap more envy for her escort. Ben was being breathtakingly attentive, of course, and that was responsible for all those envious glances. But all those other women didn't know how hateful he could be, did they?

'You are exquisitely beautiful,' he said in that smooth dark voice as he dribbled champagne into her glass. She coolly ignored him.

The table they had been given was candlelit, relatively secluded, an elegant retreat for lovers. Only they weren't lovers. Not now, not ever. And she wasn't going to let those magic bubbles go to her head, or allow his empty compliments, the way he was eating her with his eyes, soften her up. She wasn't going to be led into that kind of danger again.

From now on the barricades were well and truly up; he would not breach them again. And when he said, 'Shall we start over, Honey? Wipe out the past few weeks—because they were nonsense, you know that, don't you?' she gave him a haughty smile and countered,

'I think we should draw up a few ground rules, if that's what you mean. And stick to them.' She pushed some food around her plate with her fork. She didn't know what it was because she couldn't remember what she'd ordered from the elaborate menu. And she wished her eyes wouldn't keep going to his mouth because when they did she remembered exactly how they had felt when he had smothered her with burning kisses and she had so greedily returned them.

'Not entirely.' His gleaming eyes were reaching right into her soul and if she weren't very careful she would find herself asking what he did mean, forget that from now on in she was the one who would be calling all the shots. 'Here——' He forked up a morsel of the food from her plate and slowly inserted it into her mouth. Delicious, lip-licking prawns in a sauce that tasted of butter and sherry.

He was deadly and dangerous and everything was rapidly getting out of hand, and she had to remember he was a liar, and devious, and cruel when the mood took him. She popped another prawn into her mouth, no intimate help from him this time, and hardened her heart, making quite sure it wouldn't turn to marshmallow again.

'No? Well, whatever——' she lifted palely gleaming shoulders '—what I'd really like to talk about is the possibility of my taking over the house we're in when you leave. I shall have to live somewhere, and it might as well be there. There's little point in going through the hassle of moving all over again.'

'Out of the question,' he murmured, leaning back, steepling his fingers and looking slightly amused. Honey bit down on her lip in annoyance. He was back to patronising her again, treating her as if she were a backward child.

'Why is that? I shall have to live somewhere when we split up,' she reminded him, making herself keep cool.

'And you've no plans to go back to living above the shop.'

It wasn't even a question. She itched to slap that smugly superior expression off his face but wasn't going to give him the satisfaction of knowing that as far as her emotions were concerned he could whistle up a storm with the mere upward drift of one dark brow. So instead of giving herself the pleasure of doing something violent she said coldly, 'If you're fishing for compliments then yes, your idea of turning my living space into extra show-rooms was a good one. The customers browse much longer now they can actually move around, and more of them buy. So go to the top of the class. And as you believe you know everything there is to know about anything, perhaps you'd explain why I can't stay on when you leave.'

She was handling the situation well, she congratulated herself. She was staying cool and calm and not even he could guess at the agitation that was seething away beneath her collected exterior.

'It's quite simple,' he told her smoothly, idly waving away the waiter as he approached with the lavish dessert trolley. 'The owner is only interested in short lets. His son's getting married soon and the house is to be his wedding gift to the happy couple.'

'How soon is soon?' Honey enquired levelly, fighting panic. When they had to vacate the rented house the marriage would be officially over. He wouldn't want the trouble of setting up somewhere

else with her, carrying the pretence on for
any longer.

'I've no idea. I presume the owner will let us
know.'

'And where will that leave me?' Her temper was
rising, her agitation showing through. She no longer
cared. It was time the selfish bastard was told a few
home truths. 'With nowhere to live! You simply
pack a couple of suitcases and walk away while I'm
left with a houseful of furniture and nowhere to
put it. And we had an agreement,' she reminded
him stormily. 'So far, Graham has shown no sign
of getting involved with anyone else. What right
have you to walk away because our marriage has
served its purpose as far as you're concerned? And
you never did tell me the truth, did you? What did
you get out of it?'

'You sound as if you don't want the marriage to
end.'

'Rubbish!' For some reason his retort made her
tremble, heated colour rushing beneath her skin,
and for some reason all her stormy response did
was make him laugh, the slow dark sound of
amusement making her want to scream.

'Is it?' Speedwell-blue eyes held hers intently and
Honey's pulses fluttered unbearably. No matter
how she tried she couldn't look away.

He disturbed her without even having to try,
dominated her, did he but know it. And his lovemaking had, just briefly, made her believe an impossible lie. She wasn't in love with him, of course
she wasn't. Subsequent events had demonstrated

the impossibility of that. It had been the biggest lie she could ever have told herself!

And yet she still could not look away. She was enthralled, blinded by the fathomless depths of those incredible eyes. And when his hand reached for hers and curved over it, the blunt tips of his fingers pressing into her palm, her whole body began to burn and she couldn't have moved to save her life. And he said, his dark drawly voice sending shivers down her spine, 'Why don't you admit you want me? Admit we'd make a hell of a partnership in bed? We are married; it wouldn't even be immoral!'

Her eyes dropped to the sensual curve of his mouth and she was drowning in the deep dark pool of his seductive voice, almost tempted to admit she wanted him with an intensity that made her burn all over.

And, no matter how unimpressed he'd been with her to begin with, he wanted her now. Desire was flagrantly stamped on those utterly, fantastically male features. But that was all it was. Lust.

For him, the remainder of their time together would pass far more pleasurably if she agreed to share his bed. He had said no word of love. But then, why should he? she asked herself tartly, hauling herself painfully on to safer, firmer ground. Why should he tell yet another lie when he was supremely confident of his ability to master her with all that oozing sex appeal?

Sharply, she tugged her hand away from beneath his, produced a glare from somewhere, injected acid into her voice.

'Nice try. But all I want is sufficient advance notice to find myself somewhere more permanent to live! I don't want to hear tomorrow that I'm supposed to be out at the end of the week. You never did tell me what the terms of our tenancy were. And I made the mistake of not being interested.'

And if he had even the slightest inclination to suggest that their relationship could become permanent, their marriage a real one, then he would now tell her that she needn't worry, that they could look for a home of their own together.

But he didn't, of course he didn't, because nothing could be further from his mind. And all he said was, 'I don't believe you. What will it take to make you admit the truth?' He held up a hand, his eyes mocking. 'Don't tell me, I'm working on it.'

And he was laughing at her at the same time, she smouldered, prepared to walk right out of the restaurant because she felt degraded by his arrogant assumption that it was only a matter of time before her hormones would drive her into his bed.

But he hadn't finished with her yet. He had one more knife to use and he thrust it home with deadly accuracy, one brow tilted carelessly as he suggested, 'Then why don't you buy your old home? Folly Field is on the market again, or so I've been told.'

'Cruel!'

The word snaked out without her having to think about it. She had once been misguided enough to tell him how wretched she'd been when her mother had sold up the family home after her father's death. And the sneaky creep had taken that confidence and used it as ammunition, a way of wounding her because she had turned down his suggestion that they enliven the last days of their marriage by romping around in his bed!

'I couldn't begin to even think about affording it, as you must know. And if you've quite finished taking your spite out on me, I'd like to go home.' She stood up, staring straight ahead. Her tongue felt like a lump of wood as she informed him stiffly, 'It's time we brought our sham of a marriage to an end. Move out as soon as you like. Tomorrow wouldn't be soon enough.'

She might not have uttered a single word. They left the restaurant together and she wondered if he realised the impact he made on the female half of the customers. And decided he did. There was an arrogance about him that told of an inborn power, the ability to handle it and turn it to his own advantage. Always.

The knowledge unsettled her horribly. So did his silence. But he was relaxed, listening to classical music from the car radio on the drive back to Shrewsbury, apparently totally unaware of the inner tension that was threatening to rip her into tiny, hysterically screeching pieces.

And he didn't say a single thing until she began to scurry upstairs to bed, nothing about a willingness to move out, and put an end to their marriage, not even a curt refusal to go until it suited him, simply, 'If you're short of cash I'll buy your BallanTrent shares at the market price. Just say the word.' He named a sum that made all the fine hairs on her body stand on end. 'Avril's already agreed to sell. They would have come to you one day; as it is she's happy to let me—as your husband—buy them from her.'

'I don't believe you,' Honey croaked, turning back to face him.

He had bolted the outside door for the night and now he leaned lightly back against it, his face slightly shadowed. And she saw him for what he was, a dangerous, menacing predator who stalked his prey, not showing his fangs until he had manipulated them into a corner, and she repeated hoarsely, 'Mother would never sell her shares.'

'Ask her.' He shrugged, as if he didn't care whether she believed him or not. It wasn't important. And he moved further into the tiny hallway, nearer to the light that revealed the sudden iciness of his eyes, the cutting edge of the steel that had been hidden behind all that laid-back charm. 'As I said, I'm also willing to purchase yours. Sleep on it.'

'Never!' Her eyes flashed scornfully. He was a devious, calculating swine! She swung round and made her ascent of the staircase as dignified as she could. But in the seclusion of her bedroom she kicked off her shoes and paced the carpet, round and round.

So that was why he had wanted to marry her! To gain a fifty per cent holding in BallanTrent. Already he had tricked Avril into agreeing to sell hers, pretending they would stay 'in the family'. All very cosy, as far as her mother would know. The shares moving to her new son-in-law's control, and all that extra money to play with—all highly satisfactory!

Avril wasn't to know that the marriage wasn't a real one, couldn't last more than a few more weeks before divorce proceedings began. And with Avril's shares safely under his belt he had made a play for hers. And that was why he'd suggested she bought Folly Field. He knew how much the old family home had always meant to her, knew she couldn't possibly afford to buy it.

Then, with the seed planted in her mind, he had casually offered to buy her shares, naming a price that would put Folly Field easily within her means. No wonder he often seemed to be laughing at her!

Tonight he had finally shown his hand because he believed she wouldn't be able to resist the temptation. He was, she recognised, far more dangerous than she had dreamed possible.

CHAPTER EIGHT

AFTER a dreadful, restless night Honey overslept, waking with a headache and twanging nerves. Fred had a key to the shop, of course, but it wasn't like her to be late.

Another black mark to add to the many already chalked up against Ben Claremont!

And her mood wasn't made any sunnier when she ran downstairs and found Ben in the hall, sliding documents into his briefcase. He looked every inch the top executive, immaculately dressed in a dark business suit and exuding power from every pore.

While she, she freely admitted, looked a mess. Her vivid red hair was wild and wrinkly, her cream suit had been pulled on all anyhow and the only make-up she'd had time to apply was a dash of scarlet lipstick.

'You still here?' she snapped at him rudely. 'I asked you to leave, remember?' She pushed past him to take her bag from the hall table, hitching the strap over her shoulder, and he stared down at her, his narrowed eyes unfathomable.

'I'll leave when I'm ready and not before. So don't push your luck, Honey,' he warned drily, infuriating her.

The time for pussy-footing around was over, she decided on a spurt of recklessness that brought warm colour to her normally pale skin. Planting

131

herself firmly in front of the door, blocking his exit, she clamped her hands on her curvy hips and declared witheringly, 'As of this moment, I'm ending this marriage. I'll file for a divorce or an annulment—whatever. There's no point in continuing the farce.'

'No?' His sapphire eyes danced with amusement, roaming over her flushed little face, and one beautifully made hand brushed the tangle of curls away from her heated forehead, his sculpted mouth softening sensually.

'No,' Honey reiterated breathily, jerking her head away. 'And don't touch me!'

'Why not? Afraid you might get to like it too much?'

'Afraid I might be provoked to murder and mayhem!' she corrected agitatedly, hating him for touching the truth, hating herself for allowing that it was the truth.

But he couldn't read her thoughts and he would never know how he could turn her into a mass of physical needs. Taking comfort from that, she eyed him defiantly and pointed out, 'I'd rather endure Graham's pursuit indefinitely than stay married to you for one more day. Apart from anything else, you're a liar and I don't like liars.'

'Ah, yes, the deathbed grandfather.' He nodded sagely, his eyes dancing wickedly. 'I admit to a slight distortion of the truth here, but I'm not a congenital liar.'

'Aren't you? I wouldn't believe a word you said if it was carved on tablets of stone,' she huffed. 'I know exactly why you wanted marriage——'

'Oh, I don't think so,' he argued smoothly, moving closer, close enough for her to be alarmingly aware of the discreet scent of expensive cologne that mingled with the clean and tantalising maleness of him, to see the dancing silver lights in the blackly fringed speedwell eyes, the grainy texture of his skin.

She was backed against the door now and there was nowhere else to go and if he moved another muscle his lean and whippy body would be touching hers and she spat out, panicking, 'You wanted to get your sneaky hands on my BallanTrent shares.'

'Wrong.' He lifted a hand to the nape of her neck, his fingers sliding beneath her hair, and she was mesmerised, unable to move, to protect herself from this assault on her senses. 'I wouldn't need to be married to you to make a perfectly legitimate offer for your holding in the company, would I, Honey?'

'I——' In a moment he would kiss her and she knew she mustn't want it to happen and she was struggling to control her wanton need to melt into his arms again. She closed her eyes to block him out, to break the spell, finding enough will-power to fight him and herself. 'No, but Mother wouldn't have agreed to sell hers to anyone who wasn't family. You tricked her, but you won't trick me. You won't get a sniff of my shares, so you might as well concede defeat and get right out of my life.'

This close he was overwhelming her. She felt dizzy, too weak even to despise herself for her little mew of protest as his strong fingers ceased stroking her nape and slid away. She shuddered and he told her darkly, 'I haven't conceded defeat since I was in short trousers. I don't intend to begin now. See you this evening.' And lifted her out of his way, planted her down in the centre of the hall and walked out of the door, leaving her feeling utterly vulnerable.

'Mr Trent will see you now.' Henry's secretary smiled, making ushering movements and Honey sailed on through, her mouth set.

It hadn't taken her long to pull herself together and drive to the factory. BallanTrent had occupied this site since her father and Henry had first begun production and she wasn't about to see them closed down, swallowed up by the giant Claremont Electronics.

Ben, in his sneaky, devious way, had to be aiming to get control, to poach BallanTrent's customers away and close the company down, adding to the misery of local unemployment and making the company her father had been so proud of, worked so hard for, nothing more than a piece of history.

The least she could do was warn Henry.

'Honey—what a pleasant surprise!' Henry Trent rose from his desk, his plump face beaming. 'Sit down, sit down. Can I give you some coffee?'

'That would be nice.' She had expected a frosty reception, to say the least; he had grown increasingly impatient with her lack of interest in his precious son. He had to be better at hiding his feelings than she had expected him to be.

But his wrath would be boundless when she warned him of what was happening, told him that

Avril had agreed to sell her shares in the company to Ben.

After all, Henry had been desperate to see her married to Graham. Happy to blink an eye at his son's future happiness, and hers, so long as the shares could be pulled together within one family.

All she could do was assure him she wouldn't sell, that she would resist the temptation of Folly Field. In the past she had always liked Henry, but had seriously gone off him when he'd made it plain that he was determined to see her married to his son. But this thing was bigger than personal pique.

Waiting until his secretary had brought the coffee through and left, she took a deep breath and braced herself for the inevitable.

'There's no way of breaking this gently,' she told him, her huge eyes apologetic. 'So I'll get straight to the point. Mother's sold her BallanTrent shares to Ben Claremont and he's made an offer for mine. I refused, naturally,' she tacked on hurriedly, to let him know she wasn't going over to the enemy too. She steeled herself to leap to her mother's defence, willing to do it even though explaining the true nature of her marriage to Ben Claremont would be mortifying.

But the expected explosion didn't come. She couldn't remember Henry ever looking quite this affable and self-satisfied. And her eyebrows shot up beneath her wild fringe as he folded his plump hands over his paunch and gloated, 'Avril sold to your husband on my advice. Naturally, she wouldn't have taken such a step without first consulting me.'

'Your advice?' Honey could barely believe it. Did Henry know what he was doing?

'Exactly.' He puffed out his cheeks. 'I do believe this calls for a small celebration.' He heaved himself out of his chair and produced a bottle of fino and two glasses. 'Claremont and I had a highly productive discussion before your marriage. As you know, he is setting up a development unit here—all highly classified, of course—and, naturally enough, he was interested in the work we do here at BallanTrent.'

He handed her a glass of the straw-pale liquid and she set it aside. As far as she could see there was no cause for celebration at all. Quite the opposite. And, unaware of her deep reservations, Henry confided, 'To be perfectly frank, the recession was beginning to hit us badly. We needed a huge injection of capital—and when it comes packaged with Claremont's expertise in the field we'd be insane to turn it down. To have BallanTrent securely under the umbrella of a company like Claremont is exactly what we need. When he suggested buying in, during that initial discussion, I jumped at it.'

No wonder Henry had danced at her wedding when she'd fully expected him to boycott the proceedings, she thought wanly, wondering how to tell him that he was riding high on a big shiny bubble that would soon explode into nothing but a fistful of worthless, limp and tattered shreds.

And he'd had those discussions before the wedding. How long before? And why hadn't she, or Avril for that matter, as shareholders, been consulted? But they were way beyond that type of recrimination now and she gave Henry a steely look when he said cheerfully, 'He approached your mother, with my blessing, and I advised her to sell. And it went without saying that, as he's your husband, you would have no qualms about letting him buy your shares. His input—as I'm sure you'll be the first to agree—will be far more valuable than yours!'

'You think so?' Honey got wearily to her feet, warning, 'No wonder you were happy about the wedding. I thought you'd never speak to me again because I turned Graham down in the most final way possible. But you already knew you'd be able to keep everything all in the family, more or less, with the added bonus of the Claremont umbrella. But have you thought what might happen if Ben and I divorce? His loyalty—if he has any—to BallanTrent wouldn't be worth a row of beans.'

'Give me some credit, my dear!' His eyes twinkled at her over the expanse of his desk. 'I'm sure you and Ben will have a long and happy marriage but, knowing the regrettably high divorce-rate these days, I had the terms of the agreement state that he sells one per cent of the holding he's buying from Avril on to Graham. The same will happen if you sell. That way, Graham and I will gain overall control.'

'And Ben agreed?' Honey couldn't believe it. To have created Claremont Electronics, made it the international success it undoubtedly was, made himself a personal fortune that would be the envy of most, he would need to be a very sharp operator indeed as well as an acknowledged genius in his own field.

She couldn't imagine him pouring money into a company over which he had no direct control. For, despite his assumed aura of laid-back, easy charm, he could be as deadly as a rattlesnake, as she knew to her cost.

'But of course. I can show you proof, if you wish.' He was already fishing the safe keys out of his waistcoat pocket and Honey shook her head, convinced. Henry had obviously made the deal of a lifetime and she had yet to figure out why Ben had allowed it to happen.

'And my advice—my strong advice—to you is to go ahead and let your husband buy your shares. He can easily afford the outlay.' He laughed immoderately, obviously on a high. 'And the more he holds, the more his input will be. And just think what you could do with that kind of capital. You could expand your business, open new premises in other locations——'

'I'll think about it,' Honey cut him off, needing to get away. She had to figure out why Ben hadn't insisted on overall control of the company. There had to be a snag somewhere. There just had to be!

The sky had clouded over when she left the building. It looked ominously like rain. Getting into her car, she decided it didn't matter. Fred was happy to look after the shop; he wouldn't begrudge her an hour of thinking time. And she knew where she would be able to think more clearly.

Henry certainly believed he had Ben all sewn up; if he hadn't he wouldn't have advised her mother

to sell her shares and urged her to do the same.
Which meant that Folly Field was within her grasp.
With the price Ben was willing to pay she could buy
her father's family home back and still have a
comfortable amount left over. It would be something to compensate for the pain of her empty
marriage.

She gritted her teeth, admitting the pain, admitting that love couldn't be stifled to order. She'd
tried so hard to deny it, but you couldn't deny the
truth. But that didn't mean she was willing to go
along with him and allow him to make love to her.
Because, as sure as God made little apples, he would
end the marriage, walk away when it suited him;
that had been their agreement and he would stick
to it. He had shown no signs of wanting to change
it. And on that day something inside her would die.
She would not compound that type of heartache
by sharing his bed.

All she had to do was to get over him in the
shortest possible time, try to persuade him to end
their marriage sooner rather than later and, in the
meantime, put her mind on other things.

Like Folly Field. And perhaps, walking through
the deserted, quiet grounds, her mind would grow
clearer, calmer. And she would be able to work out
what to do for the best, what her father's advice
would have been.

As she turned off the main road, on to the narrow
country lanes, her brow wrinkled. What her father
would have had to say surely didn't signify, did it?
She had to make up her own mind on this, decide
for herself whether the best course of action was

to sell, or whether it might be better in the long run to hang on to her holding, even though, as Henry had so rightly pointed out, her input was nil.

But the decision was taken out of her hands as she braked the car and stared up at the glossy 'Sold' sign above her. And even as she sat there, feeling nauseous, a builders' van cornered and swept up the driveway in a cloud of exhaust fumes.

As if to suit her mood it began to rain and, her pale face set, she headed back to town. Buying the family home back had been a secret dream ever since her mother had sold it all those years ago.

If it had never seemed really achievable it hadn't made much difference; it had simply been a dream to occupy her rare idle moments, and even rarer sillier ones. But to have had it within her grasp and then to see it snatched away was cruel because she would never again be able to dream.

All she would have was the reality. She would never be able to call Folly Field her home. And she would never be able to call Ben her man, her husband and her lover. And, strangely, the latter was by far the more painful.

She parked her car next to Ben's at the end of the terrace and walked back through the pouring rain to the house they shared. It had rained all afternoon and for the first time in weeks they hadn't had a single customer. Which added to her feeling of deep depression.

Her suit and shoes were soaked as she let herself in and she went quietly upstairs, not wanting to draw Ben's attention. The less she saw of him the better. She felt too dispirited, too raw inside to be able to hold her own with him.

But he must have in-built radar, she thought agitatedly as he knocked on her bedroom door and walked right in with a steaming mug of coffee. And a hide as thick as an elephant's, she added inside her head. The last time she had spoken to him she'd been telling him to go, that their marriage was over. And here he was, relaxed as a cat in a dark-coloured sweatshirt over narrow black jeans, just as if that acrimonious exchange had never happened.

'I thought you might be ready for this.' He put the mug on top of the chest of drawers. 'It's bucketing down outside and there's some Chinese takeaway keeping warm in the oven. We'll eat when you're ready.'

Just that, nothing more, and when he left as quickly and quietly as he'd come Honey shrugged indifferently.

She was too dispirited to argue with him. Besides, now she came to think of it she'd had nothing all day apart from that coffee in Henry's office. Maybe her low feelings were partly due to lack of nourishment?

She had always coped with life's brickbats before, bouncing back like a rubber ball, she acknowledged as she stripped off her wet clothes. This type of enfeebling, enervating depression was unknown to her.

Even the double blow of her father's death and the loss of Folly Field had not flattened her like this. On the contrary, she had gone a little wild for a couple of years, defying her mother on every possible occasion, flouncing about, banging doors, playing hookey from school, staying out late...

So surely she could handle the fact that Folly Field now had new owners? After all, she had only seriously considered the possibility of selling those shares and buying the property for about ten minutes! And the enigma of Ben's seemingly altruistic rescue package for BallanTrent wasn't really her concern, especially as Henry and, presumably, Graham believed it to be the happiest of miracles.

And as for falling in love with Ben, well, the ensuing misery was all her own fault. She had always known that their marriage had been nothing more than a convenient arrangement, that nothing would come of it. Known it and accepted it. And he had never said anything that could have led her to expect more—such as a permanent commitment. He hadn't asked her to love him.

But she felt no brighter when she eventually went downstairs, shivering still despite the jeans and warm sweater she'd changed into. However, that was something a hot meal would soon cure. And Ben must have heard her coming down because he appeared with the hot dishes of food; he'd lit a fire in the tiny sitting-room, and they ate by its flickering light, and when she'd forked up the last delicious morsel he said, 'Feeling better now?' and poured brandy for them both.

Infinitely. It was the food and the fire, of course, and nothing at all to do with him. How could it be? They had barely exchanged a dozen words during the meal, simply eaten in companionable silence. Companionable?

She got rid of the sudden lump in her throat with a sip of brandy and Ben said, 'Sit by the fire and relax; I'll make coffee.'

'I'll do it.' Her conscience prodded. 'You made the meal.'

'I only had to heat it up. Besides, you look exhausted and I like to pamper you—given the chance,' he said gently, and Honey watched him walk out of the room, tears in her eyes.

He could be so wonderful when he forgot to be infuriating, she thought, blinking, then moved over to the sofa, facing the fire, staring into the dancing golden flames because she didn't want to have to think. And when he came back with the pot in one hand and two of her best china coffee-cups and saucers balanced in the other she said wanly, 'Folly Field's been sold. The new owners must be having work done. I watched a builder's van go up the drive.'

He went very still, his hands frozen in the act of placing the delicate cups and saucers on the table. And he asked tightly, 'Do you know who bought it?'

'No.' She couldn't imagine why she'd brought the subject up. It obviously hadn't given him any pleasure. He'd looked almost shocked when she'd told him. And she knew why. The bait had gone. He'd dangled the price of those shares in front of her with the suggestion that she could buy back her former home, knowing how much she regretted its loss.

So what would he dream up as bait now? she wondered, accepting the cup he gave her with a muttered thanks. Not that it mattered. Nothing mattered.

She sensed him moving around behind her and when he placed his hands on the back of the sofa she tensed. As he dipped his glossy dark head to the level of hers she put her cup and saucer down because her hands had started to shake.

'For you.' He caught her hand, placing a small square box in her palm. 'To mark our first anniversary.'

Honey twisted round, her fine brows drawn together, then regretted the mistake because his mouth was a mere whisper away from hers and his half-closed eyes were eating her soul.

'We have been married a month, or thereabouts,' he explained, his dark voice throbbing with amusement. 'Open it, see if it fits.'

Her fingers stiff, she prised the lid open, her eyes going wide as the magnificent diamond glittered at her from its heavy antique gold setting. The ring was beautiful. Perfect. It had to have cost a small fortune. And she said grimly, 'I can't possibly accept this.'

As a casual gift it was far too valuable and as a token it was a complete and utter mockery. Married one month. And what a month—it felt like forever! Yet she couldn't imagine being without him, couldn't bear to think of the anguish she would suffer when it was over, when he walked out of her life.

'Of course you can.' He was on the sofa beside her now. 'Humour me. I can afford it and it won't cost you anything to wear it.' He took the box from her unresisting fingers and slipped the ring on her finger, above the plain gold wedding-band she wore.

It looked good, more than good, and his hand curved round hers, his fingers lightly stroking the racing pulse point inside her wrist, his voice a definite caress as he told her, 'The moment I saw it I knew it was perfect for you, so let's be sensible about it—we've a long way to go together.'

Had they? How far? As far as the divorce courts. Was the valuable ring supposed to be some kind of settlement? Payment for putting up with him until he decided she need no longer bother?

As she opened her mouth to suggest all this his lips covered hers, pushing the words right out of her mind. The pressure was gentle, a soft persuasion, yet quite fatally erotic. And then his arms folded around her, gentling her, as if he expected her to panic and Honey went dizzy.

She was drowning, clinging to him now as if she would never let him go, and this was where she wanted to be. This was where she had been born to be.

The pressure increased and she answered it, because when he called to her she would come. It was inevitable. And his body was calling to her now, demanding its answer, this blind response, and his mouth left hers to trail kisses down the length of her throat, and somehow she was stretched out on the sofa, her hands eagerly caressing the impressive width of his shoulders.

'Honey——' He lifted his head, the blaze of passion in his eyes transfixing her.

She was sinking deeper and deeper, her whole body burning with delight and when he stretched out on the sofa beside her she moved to accommodate him, gasping as his hand cupped her buttocks, pulling her hard against his arousal. And his lips captured hers again with an urgency that excited her beyond bearing, making her wriggle ever closer to him, her body going boneless, softening, accepting.

His ragged breathing, the pounding of combined wild heartbeats, was savagely sweet music and when one of his hands slid beneath the hem of her sweater to take shattering possession of her breasts she arched against him, all inviting, acquiescent womanhood, her mouth curling wickedly, wantonly, her dark eyes dreamy as he buried his face in her vivid hair.

He said hoarsely, 'Now tell me you want me to go!' And her eyes went blind with misery.

The whole world of triumphant masculinity had echoed through that exclamation. Honey went rigid with distress and pain.

This was the night he had meant to seduce her. Everything—the caring, the warm fire, the hot meal, the gift of an exquisite ring—everything had been planned, leading up to this. An introduction to the delights of the flesh, an introduction that would leave her craving for more, only too willing to share his bed until he decided it was time to split.

Maybe she had become a challenge he wasn't prepared to ignore. Not many women would have had the strength of mind to resist him. So why should she be the one to dent his ego? Why should he pass up the opportunity of having a willing woman in his bed to enliven the nights that were left before their agreement came to an end?

He was moving restlessly above her now but his passion couldn't touch her. Not now. Never again.

Savagely, she bunched her fists against his chest and felt him go suddenly still. His eyes were hazed with desire as they met hers, and her mouth felt rigid as she said, 'This has gone far enough. Leave me alone.' And thought she saw a deep flare of pain, but she couldn't have done because his eyes went like blue ice and his voice was a harsh indictment as he accused,

'You wanted me. Is this the way you punish men?'

She wanted to tell him it wasn't true, that she had never, willingly, allowed any man as close to her as he had been tonight. That yes, she had wanted him, still did, and that she could love him until she drew her last breath, if she let herself.

But she wouldn't let herself. She couldn't punish herself to that extent. Sooner or later she would get over him.

'Perhaps,' she agreed, matching his coldness, but burning inside with anger and pain. She hated him for making her want him, love him.

He had moved, and she swung her legs off the sofa and dragged the ring he had given her from her finger, slapping it down on the table.

'I don't want this. I don't want any reminders. And I want you out of my life before you do any more spoiling.'

He swung round on the balls of his feet, his black brows thunderous as he asked bitterly, 'And just what am I supposed to have spoiled?'

She wanted to tell him, My whole life, damn you! but she couldn't, of course she couldn't. That would be far too revealing. So she said icily, 'My business relationship with Nick. What else?'

'I've already apologised for that.' He looked as if he didn't believe her and she couldn't endure it if he decided to probe more deeply.

She glared at him frostily. There was only one sure-fire way of getting him out of her hair and she took it, telling him, 'After talking it over with Henry, I've decided to sell you my BallanTrent shares. We both know that's what you've been after all along. So you can leave with what you wanted, as soon as you can arrange it. It can't be soon enough for me.'

'I see.' The mask of utter boredom slid over his face and she knew, without him having to spell it out, that their strangely tormented relationship— if such it could be called—was over.

And as if to emphasise his total indifference, now and in the future, he gave her a long unreadable look and walked out of the room.

CHAPTER NINE

ANOTHER wretched sleepless night. Honey got out of bed bad-temperedly, dragged her nightgown over her head and pulled on an ancient grey tracksuit then stuffed her feet into a pair of battered trainers.

It had only just turned six o'clock but she wasn't prepared to lie in bed, tossing and turning, for one more miserable moment. She'd grab herself a drink of orange juice from the fridge then take a long brisk walk down the riverbank. After that, a hot shower, a coffee, put on one of her smartest suits and she might just be able to face the rest of the day.

The tiny house was silent so Ben was obviously sound asleep. There really was no justice, Honey thought scornfully, then reminded herself that she'd promised—during those long and sleepless hours— that she absolutely would not think of him unless it was completely unavoidable.

So when she marched into the kitchen and found him there her heart lurched over with shock and she found herself saying, 'Oh!' before she could do anything about it. Like turning right round and getting the hell out of here.

He'd been staring out of the window and now he turned slowly around, his hands thrust deep into the pockets of his short towelling robe.

And he looked haggard, as if he hadn't slept a wink, his hard jawline dark with the night's growth of beard. Honey, rooted to the spot with the sheer anguish of his presence, had to force herself to back out. But he stopped her, his voice grim as he instructed, 'Don't go. I would like a word. It won't take more than a few minutes.'

Even a few moments in his company would be too many. Being together in the same room hurt much too much. But she had to be adult about this; it was the only way she would be able to survive the pain of loving him, the anguish of knowing that all he had wanted from her, on a personal level, had been a few romps between the sheets, the sheer awfulness of knowing that it wouldn't be long before he went away and she would never see him again.

'And don't worry, I won't try to touch you,' he told her irritably as she still hovered, half in the room, half out of it. 'I won't make that mistake again. I'm not a masochist.'

Her face miserable, she sidled in and perched herself on the nearest chair, not trusting her legs because she was suddenly shaking all over.

She had never seen him look like this. His slitted eyes were cold and deadly, his mouth a grim line. This was a side he must show to his business rivals, employees who had not quite managed to live up to the high standards he demanded, anyone who had had the temerity to displease him.

Suddenly, she longed quite desperately for that slow, effortless smile, for the silver gleams of inner amusement in those shockingly blue eyes, for the warmth and care he had shown her at times—even for one of those flashes of dry wit at her expense.

Never again would he call her his 'little nest of vipers' and even that prospect seemed impossibly doleful. He was certainly making it plain that there was now an unbridgeable distance between them and that, for him at least, presented no problem at all.

Because his voice was flatly indifferent as he explained, 'I will see that the sale of your shares goes through at the price previously mentioned. I will fax the details through to the relevant department at head office later this morning. As for my moving out, it would be more convenient if I remained here until the new development unit is up and running— if you agree.'

She nodded bleakly. What else could she do? And he turned back to the window, as if he had no further interest in the conversation, dismissing her with, 'I'm afraid I can't give you a definite time span, but it shouldn't take too long. Divorce proceedings can start on the day I move out.'

Which hurt unbearably, although she knew it shouldn't. And to cover it, to hide all that pain, she scrambled to her feet, told him with a carefully manufactured airiness, 'No problem. If you're not able to leave before Mother goes on her cruise, I'll move into her bungalow. She'll be gone for three months. You can't possibly need more time than that.' And swept out, her heart feeling as if it might burst inside her.

* * *

'Now you will drag yourself away from that shop of yours for a couple of hours to help me shop for new clothes for my cruise, won't you?' Avril persisted, just to make sure, and Honey replied tiredly, sitting down at the desk at the rear of the shop, mentally preparing herself for another of her mother's prolonged telephone conversations,

'I've already said I would. I'll pick you up next Wednesday at ten. And I'll give you lunch at that new Italian restaurant. Fred and his wife have been there and they can't recommend it highly enough.'

'Oh, him,' Avril disparaged. Whenever she came into the shop she looked at Fred as if he were a member of some unmentionable subspecies and made Honey want to hit her. 'Well, I suppose it will do. And talking of eating out, when are you and your nice new husband going to invite me to dine with you?'

Never, Honey said inside her head, then came up with what she thought her mother wanted to hear.

'You'll have to be patient. Ben's out most evenings.' Every evening since they'd had that final bust-up. Business dinners, she supposed. He wasn't the type to drive aimlessly around or sit on a park bench until he thought she'd be in bed and safely out of the way. There was nothing aimless or cowardly about him.

'Of course,' Avril purred quickly. 'I know how hard he's working to get his new business thingy settled. And he's been having a great many discussions with Henry and Graham, but of course you'll know all about that.'

She knew nothing of the kind. She hadn't seen him for days and days. He was always out of the house before she got up in the morning. And he was rarely back before the small hours, she knew that, because no matter how quietly he came into the house she always woke up.

'We'll talk on Wednesday,' Honey said, hoping her mother would get off the line. Any minute now she would have to lie and say half a dozen customers were in the shop, clamouring for attention.

But Avril was not so easily deflected; once she got talking she didn't know when to stop. And now she said brightly, 'Have you heard? Folly Field has been sold at last. Imagine! Who could want that barn of a place? I called into the estate agents' office—I explained who I was, of course—but they wouldn't tell me who the purchaser was.'

'I don't blame them,' Honey said snappily, unable to hide her reaction because just thinking about more strangers living in the family home still had the power to make her react irrationally. 'Anyway, I didn't think you were interested. You were quick enough to wash your hands of it after Dad died!'

The speaking silence on the line made Honey instantly regret her words and Avril at last said huffily, 'There's no need to be like that. You always tried to make me feel guilty. When you started behaving so badly, after we'd moved out, Dr Anderson said it was your way of getting your own back.'

'I know, and I'm sorry. Forget it now; I have.'
She wasn't being strictly truthful but she no longer
blamed Avril. Folly Field had never been right for
her. She was happier in a more compact home—
with the right touches of luxury, of course. She
needed to be within easy reach of the shops and
restaurants, the dainty coffee-shops where she could
meet up with her cronies and spend hours eating
cream-cakes and gossiping.

So no, she had learned not to blame her mother.
She had only been acting in character. But Honey
wished things had been different.

'Well, yes,' Avril agreed. 'Let bygones be bygones, that's what I always say.' Which was news
to Honey because her mother enjoyed nothing
better than chewing over her daughter's mis-
demeanours, past and present, real and imagined,
and she was still smiling wryly when that lady went
on, 'And I have to give credit where it's due. You
did very well for yourself when you married dear
Ben.'

Thanks a bunch, Honey said to herself when her
mother finally got off the line. She would be in for
a nagging beyond compare when the news of the
divorce became public knowledge, a constant
carping nagging that would last as long as her
mother had breath in her body!

It didn't bear thinking about and added considerably to her mood of depression.

And even though she was kept busy for the remainder of the day, the brisk business didn't do
much to lighten her heart and as she dragged herself

home that evening she wondered if her old optimism and buoyancy, her deep enjoyment of her chosen career, would ever return.

Of course it would, she snapped at herself as she let herself into the silent house. As soon as Ben had the new production unit off the ground he would go and their unreal marriage could be ended.

Just as soon as things were tidied up she would be able to put him right out of her mind and get on with her life. Nothing was surer than that!

But the house wasn't as silent as she'd first thought. Someone was moving around upstairs.

Ben?

Who else? An intruder would be more furtive, surely? Her vivid head tilted, she looked at the stairs, strangely reluctant to go up and find out. If Ben had decided to break the routine of the past few days and spend the evening here then she would have to go out.

The prospect of shutting herself in her room for hours, doing nothing—even her paperwork was, for the first time ever, bang up to date—didn't appeal in the slightest. And she couldn't spend time with him. The way he had turned into a distant stranger hurt her unbearably.

Though it shouldn't, of course. Why should she ache inside because he was having some kind of male tantrum, making her suffer because it was one way of soothing his dented ego?

His behaviour only went to prove that, basically, most men were the same. All they were interested in was sex, as she knew from bitter experience. If they couldn't get the female fancy of the moment between the sheets then they got all miffed and hateful. And Ben was no different!

But she had forgotten about the power of love because when he appeared at the head of the stairs and began to descend the pain came back with frightening intensity and her eyes felt too big for her little pale face and the lump in her throat was enormous.

His crisp dark hair was still slightly damp from the shower he had obviously taken and he was wearing a superbly cut dark suit, his white shirt contrasting dazzlingly. He looked spectacular and she didn't know what to say to him, because there was nothing left to say, was there?

And somehow, over the past days, his devastating good looks had transmuted to a dark, brooding arrogance and the brilliant blue eyes had lost their humour, become piercingly remote.

Jerkily, she stepped back as he drew level with her, and her breath was clogged up in her lungs. He gave her a hard look from cold eyes, seemed about to say something, then obviously changed his mind, heading for the door.

This was ridiculous! Honey thought wildly. Not talking to each other, like a couple of kids who had fallen out. And she snapped out resentfully, 'Another business dinner?'

He did turn back then but he didn't seem to see her. For him, quite obviously, she no longer existed. And just to show him she didn't care, that she hadn't asked because she wanted to know, that what he did was of no particular interest to her, she said drily, 'Then I won't bolt the door before I go to bed. I expect you'll be late again.'

And he answered expressionlessly, 'Very probably.' Then he added abruptly, as if he found having to communicate with her at all utterly distasteful, 'I'll be moving out a week from today. And I've been in touch with the owner and you can stay here until the end of the next month; the rent's paid until then. You'll be hearing from my solicitor regarding the divorce.'

He swivelled round on the heels of his polished, hand-crafted Italian leather shoes and walked out and Honey was left staring at the space where he had been, wondering how she could stay upright, continue breathing, when her heart had just curled up and died.

And she was standing there still, staring blankly at nothing, when the phone in the kitchen began to ring. On automatic pilot, she went through on legs that felt as if they had been carved from stone, and programmed reflexes alone made her pick up the receiver.

Sonia said, 'Are you alone? Could you possibly manage to pop out and meet me? We could have a meal—or would that be difficult?'

Was she implying that Ben was a monster, keeping her firmly under lock and key? Honey couldn't be bothered to ask, and Sonia gushed on, 'Colin's away on a business thing and I'm going spare, kicking my heels around an empty house. Besides, I've got something important to tell you.

It's not the sort of thing we can discuss on the phone, and that new Italian place is excellent; I've already been a couple of times.'

Honey's initial instinctive reaction was to refuse, to end the conversation and take herself off to bed, to curl up in a ball and give in to this bleak depression. But she couldn't let herself do that. Somehow she had to get on with her life and she might as well start now. So she said with a manufactured brightness that didn't quite ring true, 'What time shall I see you? Half an hour?' and Sonia screeched,

'Oh, super!' as if she were about to expire with excitement. 'I just knew you wouldn't be heavily involved with being all domestic for Ben's benefit! Half an hour it is, at the restaurant. You know where it is?'

Honey assured her that yes, she did, and replaced the receiver, her fine brows drawn together. Sonia obviously had some local tittle-tattle she couldn't wait to pass on, which would account for the invitation in the first place, the screech of excitement when she, Honey, had agreed to meet her. Gossip, especially if it could be called even remotely scandalous, was meat and drink to her old schoolfriend.

But how had she been so sure that she and Ben weren't involved in preparing an intimate dinner for two? As far as anyone else knew, and that definitely included Sonia, the two of them were still newly-weds and it would naturally be presumed that they would want to spend every available moment alone together.

Shrugging, she decided it didn't matter. Soon it would be common knowledge that she and Ben were seeking a divorce. The brevity of their marriage would be a nine-day wonder and even Graham wouldn't present a problem.

Henry had wanted, through his son, to secure her shares but he and Ben had worked out a far better deal as far as the company was concerned. So Graham would be free to look elsewhere for a wife. He had never felt anything other than mild, brotherly affection for her anyway, and had only wanted to marry her because his father had told him he must.

She didn't feel in the mood to go out, especially not with Sonia. But she really did have to force herself. She mustn't let depression gain too firm a stranglehold.

Even so, her resolve didn't carry her as far as bothering to get changed. The suit she had worn to work would do. And her feet felt like lead as she walked up through the town to the new restaurant everyone seemed to be talking about.

At least she would be able to give the place the once-over. It if didn't come up to Avril's exacting standards they would lunch elsewhere on Wednesday, somewhere tried and trusted. But, entering the restaurant, she was immediately aware that even her mother would not be able to fault the ambience.

Restrained elegance, not a candle in a wicker-clad Chianti bottle in sight, and Sonia waved to her from a table near the centre of the room and her first words were, 'Thank heaven we decided to meet early! I got the last free table—the other empty ones are all reserved. They must be doing a bomb! Mind you, so they should—the food's fantastic. Genuine Italian stuff, all freshly made, nothing out of packets or tins. You can tell, can't you? And I ordered you a nice G and T; drink it up while we plough through the menu. We'll splurge out on a bottle of Frascati to have with our meal, shall we? Goodness, you look peaky!'

Honey dutifully took a sip of her gin and tonic, her blank eyes fixed on the huge paste brooch pinned to the shoulder of the bright emerald-green dress her friend was wearing. She had hardly taken in a word Sonia had said and began to wish she hadn't forced herself to come. She knew she would find it almost impossible to concentrate on all that non-stop chatter and, although Sonia was shallow, she wasn't a fool and would quickly pick up on the heavy depression she simply couldn't shake off.

Her fears were realised earlier than she had expected when the other woman told her, 'I said you're looking peaky! You should have told me if you didn't feel well. We could easily have done this another time.'

'I'm sorry.' Honey forced a smile and hoped it wasn't too bleak. 'I'm fine. We've been so busy just lately, you wouldn't believe. And I've had a spate of auctions to look in on.' And swallowed the rest of her drink. If alcohol would lift her depression a little she might be able to get through the evening. She buried herself in the menu, making what she hoped were bright comments, and ordered something she'd never heard of and hoped she'd be able to force some of it down.

'If hard work makes you look like a wet weekend, you should pack it all in,' Sonia advised as the waiter moved away. 'You don't need to work, after all. Ben's loaded, everyone knows that. He could easily afford to keep you in the manner to which you would like to become accustomed—without your having to lift a finger!'

Honey looked up and met the other woman's hard, glittering eyes. There was a look of suppressed excitement about her, something she was having difficulty bottling up. And she knew her own face had gone bleak at the mention of Ben's name; it felt tight and pinched as it had done for days now, and Sonia said, with spurious concern, 'Oh, darling—I'm so sorry! Do you want to talk about it?'

'Talk about what?' She tried to look mildly amused but was horribly afraid she was only projecting misery. Sonia smiled stealthily, pouring wine from the bottle that had just arrived at their table.

'Drink up. It might help. Truly.' She rested her elbows on the table, lowering her voice. 'I know Ben's been playing around. That's what I needed to talk to you about—to warn you. But you can't hide it from me; we know each other far too well. You already know, don't you, my poor sweet?'

'You're off your trolley!' Honey managed a tired smile. She knew Sonia's addiction to tittle-tattle, her inability to keep a still or discreet tongue in her head. And if there happened to be no gossip to pass round the whispering circuit she wasn't above making something up!

Besides, up until a few days ago, Ben had been too busy trying to seduce her into his bed to have time to play around with any other woman!

Mercifully, Sonia kept silent as their order was brought to the table but as soon as the waiter was out of earshot she stated with just a hint of malice, 'Pardon me—but I know what I've seen with my own eyes, darling! Right here, too.'

'And what was that?' She really wasn't much interested but felt the question was expected of her, and, as she'd known, the other woman was immediately mollified.

'I was lunching here with a couple of girlfriends a few days ago and who should walk in but Ben. Complete with a tall, quite beautiful blonde. Well, naturally, I didn't think much of it at the time. I mean, she could have been a colleague or something. Mind you, they looked very—well, close, if you know what I'm getting at. And when I went over to have a chat I could tell he wasn't pleased to see me!'

That figures, Honey thought tiredly as Sonia paused to fork up a mouthful of food. Most people ran a mile when they saw Sonia coming because once she latched on she wouldn't let go. And the woman, whoever, could have been a colleague.

'And he didn't bother to introduce us. I mean—
after the hospitality Colin and I gave him! He
looked all annoyed the way men do when they get
embarrassed. Mind you, I got my own back! I made
a point of inviting him to dinner, after Colin's home
from his business thing. And I said, quite clearly,
"And bring your wife—it's simply ages since I saw
her. And she is my oldest, dearest friend!" And,
my dear, he didn't turn a single hair. Neither did
she. Too, too brazen!'

'Fancy!' Honey said drily. Honestly, it was too
much! She had decided, much against her inclination, to spend the evening with Sonia, believing
that her idle prattle would stop her thinking about
Ben, be the first step in taking charge of her own
life again, stop her mooning and mourning over
her misfortune—the crass stupidity of falling in love
with him—and the wretched woman hadn't stopped
talking about him!

'And then, the evening before last——' she was
in full flood again, talking up a storm between quick
sips of wine and bites of food '—Colin and I came
here. He was leaving on his business thing the next
morning, so we were early. Just before we left, who
should come in but—well, I don't need to tell you,
do I? My dear—she looked utterly ravishing! And
while Colin went to the little boys' room I turned
and gave them such a look! Well deserved, too. He
was holding her hand, right in full view of everyone!
And the way they were talking together, well,
anyone could see what was going on. And another
thing,' she babbled on, as if she hadn't said enough

to make her point. 'While Colin was settling up, I had a word with one of the waiters. The short fat one. I asked if Mr Claremont and his companion came here regularly. And he said yes, quite often, recently——

And on the night of his first 'business dinner' weeks ago he had taken his blonde companion to the Rainbow Fleece, Honey thought bleakly, no longer listening.

She had waited up for him, had wondered how a mere business occasion could have stretched on so long. And after that he had turned his lustful attentions to her, finding her a challenge. And when she'd let him know that she had no intention of ending up in his bed he'd decided she wasn't worth the hassle and had gone back to the blonde, whoever she was. Well, that figured.

Always providing, of course, that Sonia wasn't making a mountain out of a molehill.

She cut firmly across whatever Sonia was saying. 'And what did Colin have to say about Ben and the mysterious blonde? After all, he must have seen them together too.'

'You know men!' Sonia dismissed. 'Whatever happens, they'll stick together. Anyway, what are you going to do about it?'

'Nothing.' Honey felt like an old limp dishcloth. What could she do?

On the one hand, theirs hadn't been a normal marriage and on the other the woman could have been a colleague. She and Ben could have been having perfectly ordinary business discussions, with

Sonia supplying all the salacious extras. In any case, she thought drearily, what did it matter? It wasn't as if theirs had been a real marriage, a love match, and she had lost him to another woman. You couldn't lose what you had never had.

'Aren't you even going to tackle him?' Sonia wanted to know, looking as if she couldn't believe her ears, and Honey applied herself to her rapidly cooling meal, couldn't get beyond one mouthful and swallowed her wine instead.

'I may mention it,' she conceded coldly. 'There's probably a perfectly innocent explanation.' And even if there were, Sonia wouldn't believe it; as soon as the divorce became public knowledge she would have a ball and the news that ever since that brief honeymoon Ben had been flagrantly unfaithful would be around town like wildfire. She put her glass down on the table and reached for her bag, determined to get out of here before another word was said.

'I really must go. And thank you for your concern, but it really was misplaced.' At least she had come through the ordeal with dignity, she thought, and if she hadn't been feeling so low and utterly miserable she would have laughed aloud at the look of dismay that made Sonia's mouth fall open.

'But we haven't had coffee!'

'No. But I must go; I am rather tired.' And that was the truth. A heavy weariness was creeping all over her. All she wanted to do was forget. Forget she had ever met Ben, married him and fallen in love with him. And when Sonia said huffily,

'Can I go to the little girls' room, or are you in too much of a rush?' she merely nodded her head and beckoned the waiter over. She would pay the bill, wait for the other woman in the lobby and then creep home to bed and hope for the blessed oblivion of sleep.

The bill settled, she turned to walk to the lobby that separated the main restaurant from the street and walked straight into Ben. And the woman.

And Sonia had been right. She was utterly ravishing. She was tall and willowy with the type of blonde fragility that would drive most men wild. Her slanting eyes were the colour of bruised pansies and her mouth a lush rosebud.

Honey felt her body go rigid, what little colour she had had draining away as she fixed her eyes on Ben's hand, which was curved lightly round the woman's tiny waist.

Jealousy sliced through her with all the finesse of a rusty knife. It made her feel sick with pain. It made her bones shake.

Ben had left the house on the riverbank long before she had. What had these two been doing for all this time? The bruised, sultry look in the blonde's eyes, the full, seductive pout of her rosy mouth answered the question as far as Honey was concerned. They hadn't been having a dry business meeting, that was for sure!

'Honey——' he said her name, his voice sharp. But she wasn't hanging around to listen. Her body was rigid with tension and she couldn't breathe, but she managed to swoop out of there with her head high, gathered up a startled Sonia on the way and swept her out on to the street.

Her so-called friend had been right. Ben had been playing around with a vengeance, and she was almost too angry to speak to her but she managed to snap through her teeth, 'The bill's been paid and if you're thinking of asking I don't want you to give me a lift home.' And stormed away down the street and didn't look back.

CHAPTER TEN

JEALOUSY and rage fuelled Honey's blood supply, pumping it violently round her veins as she strode down the street in the purple evening light, grinding her teeth.

Sheer scalding anger glittered in her eyes and the depression of the past dreary days had lifted out of sight. The creature who had dragged herself wearily around, looking at life with beaten eyes, finding nothing to enjoy, nothing to strive for, had been a total wimp! She didn't even want to think about her; it made her feel ashamed!

Why should she behave as if the joy had gone out of living simply because a rotten louse had behaved like a louse? How could she have believed that because their stupid marriage was hopeless nothing mattered?

It was still hopeless, nothing had changed there, but by heaven—it mattered!

And she knew exactly what she was going to do. Her furniture would go into store tomorrow and she would move in with her mother. And if Avril said one word—one solitary word—she would strangle her!

Then she would start looking for a house to buy. She'd use the money that would be raised by the sale of those shares without a single qualm. And then she'd get on with her life, maybe expand her business.

But first...

Marching into the house, slamming the door behind her, she turned and bolted it securely. The ratfink could find himself someplace else to sleep. With the willowy blonde or in a cardboard box—that was his problem. Never again would they spend a single minute beneath the same roof!

Kicking off her shoes, she hitched up her skirt and took the stairs two at a time. Straight into his room. In no time at all she'd dragged his empty suitcases from the top of the wardrobe, opened the window and hurled them out. They met the paved area above the slow-moving waters of the Severn with a couple of satisfying clunks.

He was vile! A worm! He'd certainly kept to the spirit of their marriage agreement, but not to the letter. He'd had his affair but he had been far from discreet about it! Sonia knew, and if she knew then so would everyone else north of the Watford Gap!

And when she remembered his self-righteous anger—and its shaming aftermath—when he'd thought she and Nick had been enjoying clandestine sex, she felt mad enough to murder! Vile hypocrite!

Dragging her fingers through her wild and crinkly red hair, she sped to the wardrobe and wrenched out his beautiful suits, flinging them far out into the night. Shoes, shirts, socks—everything that came to hand—quickly followed, littering the little garden, draped over bushes, scattered over the lane.

Soon, not a single item of his would be left to foul the atmosphere. He would have no possible excuse to demand to be let in when he finally sneaked home in the early hours of the morning. He could spend a nice productive hour or two searching for all his hateful belongings!

Breathing rapidly, she pulled air in through flared nostrils, glancing round the room, her eyes lighting on his briefcase, neatly stowed between the wardrobe and the chest of drawers. Pouncing on it, she waltzed over to the window, still on an adrenalin high.

If she leaned out far enough she might be able to toss it into the water. Weeks and weeks of hard work lost in the mud of the riverbed. That would teach him a lesson he wouldn't forget in a hurry—teach him not to mess up her life!

The briefcase clasped to her heaving bosom, she leaned far out over the sill and saw him looking up at her. Shock made her mouth fall open.

Had the willowy blonde sent him packing? Had they sated their sexual appetites before they'd gone for dinner? Hadn't he felt up to a repeat performance? They must have swallowed their meal in one big mouthful!

It was almost dark now, his upturned face just a pale blur so she couldn't read his expression. But his voice sounded low and growly as he asked, 'What the hell do you think you're doing?'

'Getting rid of you!' she yelled right back at him, her face going red.

'Hooligan!'

'Adulterer!'

Hurling the briefcase at his feet, she closed the window with a definitive bang, turned her back on the wall and slid slowly down it, her legs stretched out in front of her.

All at once she felt strangely deflated. Empty. She'd used up a lot of energy during the last half-hour, she assured herself. She would get it back in no time at all. And when she did she would make herself a pot of tea and close all the curtains so that she wouldn't be able to look out and see him hunting around for all his scattered clothing.

She didn't want to witness that hunk of prime manhood losing his dignity. A tear gathered in the corner of her eye and she rubbed it brutally away.

Scrub that! She would love to see him lose his dignity, crawling around on his hands and knees in the dark, looking for his socks! On his hands and knees was where he fully deserved to be!

And, come to think of it, she had definitely expected to hear him hammering against the sturdy bolted door, trying to make her let him in.

Her ears twitched. Not a single sound. Disappointment dragged the corners of her mouth down. But that was only because she would have enjoyed hearing him uselessly beating his knuckles to a pulp!

Two more insubordinate tears flooded her eyes and she lifted her hands to dash them away and when she looked up again he was standing in the open doorway, his mouth a wry twist, one dark brow drifting upwards.

Honey's heart kicked at her ribs and her eyes went wide. How had he got in? Magic? And then she remembered the back door. Oh, why hadn't she thought to bolt that too? And he stared right back at her with narrowed eyes, drawling, 'You really let the lid off that temper of yours this time. I was beginning to believe you'd forgotten how.' His eyes were dancing with amusement, as if this were one huge joke.

Something hard and painful bunched up beneath her breast bone. Honey ignored it. Her eyes snapped at him as she scrambled to her feet.

'If you think I'm going to go into a decline, just because you believe in spreading yourself around...' Her voice tailed off, strangled. She had been doing just that, going into the mother and father of all declines. But not any more. She wasn't, was she?

Of course not. She made her mouth go tight and glared at him and couldn't believe her eyes because he was grinning. He looked as if he'd just been handed the gift of perpetual youth, all wrapped up in silver ribbons, and not at all like a man who'd come home to find all his intimate possessions scattered around the neighbourhood.

'Can't you take a hint?' she enquired, trying to sound cool. 'I don't want you anywhere near me. Don't you understand?'

He stepped right into the room, closing the door behind him, and Honey's mouth went dry. He looked magnificent and he didn't look angry. But then you could never tell with him; he was tricky and devious and sneaky and... And what if he intended to take her by the scruff of the neck and toss her out of the window too?

He gave her a look that almost melted her and then his arms folded around her and there was a definite look of triumph in his smile as he said roughly, 'You were jealous. That's the only thing I need to understand. You saw me with Emma and you were jealous.'

'Not in the least,' Honey argued defiantly, daring her treacherous body to lead her astray. The wretched thing wanted to squirm closer to him, to cling, to plead for his kisses. 'I was just annoyed.' She bunched her fists, pummelling his wide shoulders. But all that achieved was the tightening of his arms around her.

'If you create that kind of mayhem when you're "just annoyed" my darling——' his hands slid up to cup her head, his fingers splayed in the vivid wildness of her hair, his fabulous blue eyes holding hers '—then what would happen if you really got mad? World War Three?'

Those fascinating silver lights were back in the fathomless blue depths, she noticed, her entranced eyes mesmerised by his. And then she remembered what they were fighting about and she told him scornfully, 'You're disgusting. Of course I was annoyed. The whole town knows about your—your carryings-on. Sonia saw you with that—that woman.'

'And couldn't wait to tell you all about it. That figures. I'll have to buy her a big bunch of roses for services rendered.'

'Oh! Don't tell me! Not Sonia too?'

'Imbecile! What do you take me for? A super-stud? If Sonia hadn't told you about my night-time activities you wouldn't have been jealous and I wouldn't have known——' The pads of his fingers were massaging her scalp and her eyes had gone dreamy, and when he bent his head and brushed his lips over hers they closed altogether, and he whispered against her mouth, 'What do I know, Honey? Tell me.'

That she needed her head examining! That was what he knew! He was so sure he could do what he liked with her, whenever he felt like it! Her eyes flew open, glittering with self-disgust.

'Stop mauling me! Go back to that woman if you're that desperate!' She squirmed out of his arms but he hauled her back without any effort at all, dragging her down with him on to the bed.

'That woman,' he murmured, 'is one of my best development technicians. She is to be in charge of the new unit.'

'I'm so happy for her!' Honey hissed, dripping sarcasm, desperately trying to flail her way out of this. There was no way she was going to be able to disguise the way her body was responding to the closeness of his, the intimacy of being tangled together on top of the bed.

Any minute now all her control would disappear like a puff of smoke; already her hold on it was alarmingly tenuous. She couldn't believe that her wretched body was so responsive to such a louse!

Frantically, she tried to wriggle off the bed, but her action brought its own punishment as he captured her easily, his hard body pinning her against the mattress. And his breathing was as ragged as her own as he growled, 'I was glad you were jealous. When we bumped into you at the restaurant there was no mistaking it. I'd given up all hope, days ago—when you froze me off, said you were punishing me for being male. The pain in your eyes gave me back my hope.'

He rolled off her, pulling her suddenly boneless body into the curve of his, one arm cradling her head to his shoulder, the other stroking her tangled, wrinkly curls. And he murmured softly, 'There's no need for you to be jealous, not of any woman, ever. As I said, Emma's to be in charge of the new unit. She and her son, Alan, moved up here a couple of weeks ago. We've been liaising closely. And then, just under a week ago, Alan was taken into the Royal Shrewsbury with appendicitis. He's only seven years old. He had his operation a couple of days later. The situation wasn't serious enough to warrant his father asking for compassionate leave—he's a serving officer in the Navy, at present engaged on highly hush-hush manoeuvres somewhere in the gulf. So Emma has been spending all her days with Alan, then dashing back from the hospital to put in a few hours' work with me.'

His fingers had drifted to the underside of her jaw, stroking the delicate structure, and his voice was as soft as melted butter as he assured her,

'Normally, I wouldn't have dreamed of asking her to work. But when I gave up hope of ever making our marriage a real and lasting one, I had to get the job done as quickly as possible.'

The tips of his fingers slid over her neat little chin then drifted up over her lips. They parted and Honey lapped the pads with her pointed tongue and his voice went rough as he excused, 'And the least I could do, after her long days spent with Alan, the hours of work I made her put in with the computers and so on at the new site, was to give her a decent meal and help her unwind.'

Honey wriggled round, levering herself up on one elbow, and his fingers trailed down to the base of her throat. She leant forward slowly and ran her fingers through his hair and he groaned huskily, 'Had things been different between us, I would have asked you to eat with us. She could do with some female support right now. Emma's had a tough time recently, with the worry over her kid, missing her husband and trying to settle into a new home and a new job. I do my best to be supportive but it isn't the same as having another woman to talk with. She hasn't been in the area long enough to make friends.'

His hand had moved beneath her suit jacket, disposing of it without even seeming to try, his fingers parting the silky blouse she wore beneath it, and Honey could hardly hear his words for the pounding of the blood in her veins. And the power of articulate speech seemed to be leaving him because his words were quick and slightly slurred.

'I know you'll like her when you get to meet her. As soon as I told her you were my wife—after our confrontation this evening—she couldn't agree quickly enough when I suggested I put her straight in a taxi while I raced down here to tell you I love you.'

'Do you mean that, Ben?' she breathed, her eyes closing in ecstasy as his hand curved round one fully pouting, rose-tipped breast.

And he growled, 'What do you think? More than life,' and took the rosy offering between his lips; she arched her head back on her slender neck and thought she was going to die. But not yet, not quite yet!

Eagerly, she scrabbled at his shirt buttons, desperately needing to touch him. He loved her! She loved him! And oh, could they ever get close enough?

'Easy——' He captured both her wrists, leaning over her, forcing her back against the pillows. 'You're not going to try to freeze me off again? I warn you, I won't be responsible if you do.'

'Oh, no,' she breathed, all melting big brown eyes and parted, sultry lips. 'I'm all yours, every bit of me, now and always. I've loved you for ages,' she told him, suddenly serious. 'But I thought you just wanted a woman in your bed. I thought you'd walk away from the marriage as easily as you'd walked into it. It would have killed me if you had—if I'd gone to your bed, as I wanted to.'

'You wanted to?'

'Of course. I loved you, I just told you that.'

His eyes crinkled. 'So you did. But every time I got near to breaking through those reserves, you froze me off. Sonia had said you were a man-hater at heart.'

'Sonia said!' She snapped up against the pillows. 'I could strangle that woman. What does she know about anything? Let me tell you,' she said severely, 'I'm as normal as the next woman! I just don't like being pawed around. I don't like men who take it for granted that dinner for two automatically reserves a place in my bed! I'm particular, not peculiar!'

'I'm glad to hear it.' He was kneeling up, facing her, his eyes holding hers with a smile, and a bubble of laughter rose up inside her to meet the laughter in his eyes. And then it died.

'There is more than that,' she confessed, her small face solemn. 'After Dad died and Mother sold the house, I got a bit mixed up. Wild, you know?' He nodded, his face very still, watching her closely, and she went on, her voice carefully level, 'Mother said I was trying to make her feel guilty, and I believe it. Among other stupid things, I began going around with a crowd of bikers. Black leather and all that stuff. I thought they were my friends. I thought they were adult—without being rigid and censorious like my mother and my teachers. I thought they cared about me as a person, about my feelings and my rights. But one night, after a disco—to which, I may add, I'd been forbidden to go—three of them dragged me outside. It would have been rape if a man and woman, walking their dog, hadn't come along.' She shook her head. 'I was so gullible. I thought they were my friends. I would have trusted them with my life.'

'And ever since then you've been wary of men, or wary enough to see every attempt at lovemaking as a denial of friendship, of caring?' He gently stroked away the tangle of hair that had fallen forward to cover her face.

'You could be right.' She frowned, dragging the edges of her blouse together and he didn't touch her, he simply said quietly, 'Don't hide your body, Honey. Let me look at you.'

Flickering a glance at him beneath lowered lids, she saw the love on his face and smiled softly, almost shyly, and let her hands drop. The blouse parted again and her smile grew dreamy as she watched the way his eyes caressed her as he murmured, 'Sex, without love, is a pretty meaningless thing, my darling. Unfortunately for you, in view of what happened to you, you were blessed with the type of face and body that make most red-blooded males want to bed you. I'm not surprised you had to fight them off. But when people love, truly love, then it's not merely sex. It's the most beautiful, the greatest commitment to each other that lovers can make. But I think you already understand that, don't you, Honey?'

He opened his arms to her and she melted into them, her smile radiant, loving him, wanting him too much to do more than nod her bright head as he whispered, 'Let me show you just how beautiful it can be.'

*　　*　　*

'Better?' Ben caressed her hand as it lay limply on the kitchen table and she smiled at him dreamily. Her man, her lover, her beautiful husband.

An hour earlier, at three in the morning, Ben had whispered drowsily in her ear, 'I'm going to make bacon and eggs. Want some?'

Slowly, they had untangled their limbs, creeping hand in hand down to the kitchen and she had cooked while he had watched her, devouring her body in its clinging silk robe with hungry eyes.

And his eyes were still hungry and she knew that soon he would carry her back to heaven again, way, way beyond the glittering stars. But she wanted to know, had to know, 'When did you first know you loved me?'

'The moment I saw you.'

He saw doubt and distress cloud her lovely eyes and tightened his grip on her hand when she objected stiffly, 'Before we married you told me I didn't turn you on. You made a point of telling me.' Her soft mouth trembled. 'So you couldn't have loved me at first sight. You lied.'

'That I freely admit.' Her hand stiffened within his and he gave it a tug. 'Come here,' and hauled her to her feet, pulling her on to his lap.

He had dragged on his suit trousers when they'd come down to eat and she held herself rigidly, well away from that broad expanse of olive-toned skin. She didn't want him to have lied to her.

'I'd heard all about you from chatterbox Sonia, remember? She was quite sure that you'd do the right thing and accept Graham, eventually. You weren't interested in men, but, from a business viewpoint, marriage between you was possible, even desirable. It was only a matter of time before you accepted the sense of such an agreement, in her opinion. And when I saw you I knew you were the one woman I'd been waiting for all my life, the only woman I could share my future with. I couldn't go through a lengthy courtship. For one thing I didn't have the time. You told me yourself what pressure you were under—you could have decided to settle for Graham, just for the sake of peace. And on the other hand, how could I get near you when you were so determined to keep the entire male sex at arm's length?'

He felt her begin to relax and curved her into his body.

'So I told you I'd come up with this great idea. A marriage in name only. It would get you off the hook as far as Graham went, but I had to come up with some reason for wanting to tie myself down. After all, as far as you were concerned, we were almost strangers. While I felt I'd known and loved you all my life. So I lied about having a sick old grandfather and the threatened inheritance. I would have perjured my soul for the opportunity, the time, to get you to love me. I needed to create a situation where I would have time and you wouldn't feel threatened. But that, I promise, is the only lie I've told you, or will ever tell you. And soon we'll take that honeymoon, visit my parents and my grandfather. You're the one woman in the world who could hold her own with the old curmudgeon.'

He gentled her head down into the arch of his shoulder, stroking her hair.

'I said you don't turn me on because it's too meaningless and trite a description for what I feel. You don't "turn me on", you ravish my senses, you exhilarate me; you are my completion, you walk through my days and haunt my dreams, you fill my heart and enrich my soul. I can't begin to tell you what you mean to me.'

Tears of happiness were trickling unashamedly down her cheeks and he kissed them lovingly away, then, standing up, he cradled her in his arms.

'Time to go back to bed, my lovely. You need adequate rest. I expect you to be up at first light, rescuing my clothes. You threw them out, you can bring them back in.'

But they got very little rest. And just before dawn Ben fell asleep, his head against her breasts. Honey ran gentle, loving fingers over his hard jawline, the stern line of his nose, the sensuous curve of his mouth, then gradually, carefully, eased herself off the bed.

It was still difficult to believe how generous fate had been. This time yesterday she had been so close to losing him. She shuddered suddenly, knowing how bleak her life would have been if he had left her, if they had never confessed their deep and abiding love for each other.

But she wasn't going to think that way. Their life together would be full of good things, the best things—love, desire, understanding and plain old-fashioned liking—things that would bond them closer together with every day that passed.

Silently, she padded out of his room and into hers, knowing that separate rooms were a thing of the past, and dressed quickly in jeans and a light sweater, pushing her feet into her old trainers before she quietly ran downstairs.

Stepping out into the tiny garden, she filled her lungs with sweet fresh air. Mist was swirling above the river, softening the outline of the trees on the opposite bank while the sky was a delicate pearly pink. A new day. A brand-new beginning. Her heart felt as though it would burst with happiness.

Then, clucking at her own rampaging folly, she began to scoop up Ben's belongings. Oh, how could she have done such a thing? Everything would be ruined! Feverishly, she tried to smooth the creases from a dew-dampened pair of immaculately tailored trousers that had spent the night festooned over the garden gate, and yelped as a spider ran out of one of the pockets.

And from behind her Ben said, 'That's what I like to see—a dedicated penitent.'

She spun round to face him, her eyes sparkling. 'I thought you were asleep. Will you ever forgive me?' she asked, knowing he would.

'That depends on how repentant you are.' He came to her, folding her into his arms, whispering against her lips,

'I reached for you and you weren't there.'

All he was wearing was a low-slung towel and her hands caressed his back, loving the warm satin feel of his skin beneath her palms, the hard muscle and bone, and he told her huskily, 'I was going to help you but on second thoughts you can gather the debris on your own. It will be good for your soul, if not your temper! The next time you're tempted to throw things you'll remember that I'll be around to make you pick up the pieces.' He twirled her around, tapping her neat bottom. 'Go. I'll make the tea. And when you've picked up every last thing I'll tell you about our new home. I think you've heard of it. Folly Field.'

It couldn't be! Twirling round, her eyes very wide, she saw the door close behind him. Oh, the aggravating creature! Her eyes sparkled. He was aggravating—but so wonderful with it! And her smile didn't wear off, even though her back was breaking as she scooped up the very last sock and added it to the untidy bundle in her arms. And she was breathless as she dumped the lot on the kitchen table and enquired demurely, 'Do you want a detailed inventory?'

'An inventory is definitely not what I want at this moment. Would you like a cup of tea?'

'No.'

'Good. Neither would I. What about a nice lie down?'

'Yes, please. Oh, Ben, I do love you!'

'Good. As I'm going to have to spend the day in bed—strangely enough I haven't anything fit to wear—I'd like you to keep me company. We can talk about our new home. You are sure you like the idea?'

'Then you did buy it—you really did!' She hurled herself into his arms, wrapping herself around him. 'When?'

'As soon as I realised how much it meant to you. I'd do anything to make you happy. You know that, don't you?'

He kissed her with a savage hunger that made her mind whirl and for some time after she nestled against him, too ecstatic to speak. And then she reminded him breathily, 'You were cruel. You offered to take over those shares so that I could afford to buy the house. But you already knew it was no longer for sale.'

'Did I?' He tilted her chin, holding her eyes. 'The one wasn't meant to be contingent on the other. I mentioned the possibility of your getting your old home back because I wanted to be absolutely sure you still wanted it. I'd already put in my offer, I was still hoping our marriage would end up as a real one. The house was to be my wedding gift to you.'

'Ah, Ben.' Her eyes melted with adoration and she probed softly, 'And if things hadn't gone the way you planned?'

'It would still have been yours,' he told her gently, one brow drifting upwards as he asked, 'You're not going to tell me to sling my hook now you know Folly Field's yours, either way?'

She shook her head, her bright hair dancing. 'We could live in a garden shed and I would still be blissfully happy. When I saw that ''Sold'' sign I was disappointed. But only because it was the end of a pretty childish dream. What was hurting me most at the time was knowing I was soon to lose you. And will you tell me why you settled for forty-eight per cent of the shares in BallanTrent? It's right out of character.'

'Don't you believe it!' His eyes glinted at her. 'The Trents may have more voting clout but I hold the purse strings. They'll do as I say, without a murmur. They both understand that if they don't I'll pull the rug out from under their feet. And if you're ever tempted to wonder if I married you to get enough leverage to buy up Avril's shares, and yours, then forget it. I'd already decided to buy into BallanTrent long before I met you. It was one of the things that led to my decision to set up the new development unit in this area. Now——' He reached for her, pulling her closer, and demanded huskily, 'Come with me. We can continue these endless discussions far more comfortably if we're tucked up in bed.'

He lifted her and she wound her arms around his neck, trailing kisses along his rough jawline. And she knew there would be no more discussions, not for ages. There was nothing to talk about, only love, and that in abundance, and she would be more than content with that. Always.

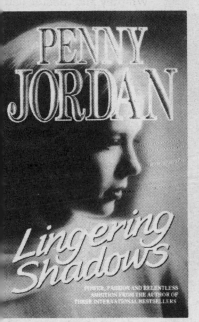

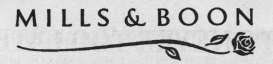

MILLS & BOON

Forthcoming Titles

DUET
Available in April

The Betty Neels Duet **A SUITABLE MATCH**
THE MOST MARVELLOUS SUMMER

The Emma Darcy Duet **PATTERN OF DECEIT**
BRIDE OF DIAMONDS

FAVOURITES
Available in April

NOT WITHOUT LOVE Roberta Leigh
NIGHT OF ERROR Kay Thorpe

LOVE ON CALL
Available in April

VET IN A QUANDARY Mary Bowring
NO SHADOW OF DOUBT Abigail Gordon
PRIORITY CARE Mary Hawkins
TO LOVE AGAIN Laura MacDonald

Available from W.H. Smith, John Menzies, Volume One,
Forbuoys, Martins, Tesco, Asda, Safeway and other paperback
stockists.

Also available from Mills & Boon Reader Service,
Freepost, P.O. Box 236, Croydon, Surrey CR9 9EL.

Readers in South Africa - write to:
Book Services International Ltd, P.O. Box 41654,
Craighall, Transvaal 2024.

Next Month's Romances

Each month you can choose from a wide variety of romance with Mills & Boon. Below are the new titles to look out for next month, why not ask either Mills & Boon Reader Service or your Newsagent to reserve you a copy of the titles you want to buy – just tick the titles you would like and either post to Reader Service or take it to any Newsagent and ask them to order your books.

Please save me the following titles: **Please tick**

Title	Author	✓
AN UNSUITABLE WIFE	Lindsay Armstrong	
A VENGEFUL PASSION	Lynne Graham	
FRENCH LEAVE	Penny Jordan	
PASSIONATE SCANDAL	Michelle Reid	
LOVE'S PRISONER	Elizabeth Oldfield	
NO PROMISE OF LOVE	Lilian Peake	
DARK MIRROR	Daphne Clair	
ONE MAN, ONE LOVE	Natalie Fox	
LOVE'S LABYRINTH	Jessica Hart	
STRAW ON THE WIND	Elizabeth Power	
THE WINTER KING	Amanda Carpenter	
ADAM'S ANGEL	Lee Wilkinson	
RAINBOW ROUND THE MOON	Stephanie Wyatt	
DEAR ENEMY	Alison York	
LORD OF THE GLEN	Frances Lloyd	
OLD SCHOOL TIES	Leigh Michaels	

If you would like to order these books in addition to your regular subscription from Mills & Boon Reader Service please send £1.90 per title to: Mills & Boon Reader Service, Freepost, P.O. Box 236, Croydon, Surrey, CR9 9EL, quote your Subscriber No:.................................. (If applicable) and complete the name and address details below. Alternatively, these books are available from many local Newsagents including W H Smith, J Menzies, Martins and other paperback stockists from 8 April 1994.

Name:...

Address:..

....Post Code:..............................

To Retailer: If you would like to stock M&B books please contact your regular book/magazine wholesaler for details.

You may be mailed with offers from other reputable companies as a result of this application.
If you would rather not take advantage of these opportunities please tick box   ☐